WATER DRAGONS BOOK 3

CHARLENE HARTNADY

DEDICATION

To my wonderful readers.

CHAPTER 1

What the fuck am I doing here?

How had he allowed himself to be convinced that this was a good idea? It had been years and years since he had gone on a Stag Run. As expected, he was bored and frustrated and irritable. He was suddenly reminded of why he had stopped going in the first place. It was like being given a bucket of candy he would never be able to savor. It didn't matter how good the treat looked, or how delicious the thought of it was, once he put it in his mouth, he'd get…nothing. *Sweet fuck all!* It would be like sucking on a pebble. Why bother even trying? Why look?

He watched as Delta nuzzled the neck of a very willing human. Then he was groping her breast. It wouldn't be five minutes and the two of them would leave together. They would spend the night together. He'd already watched several others from the group pair up and head out. *Lucky fucks!* Bay ground his teeth, trying to look away from the couple as they continued to make out. He couldn't take his eyes off them though; call it morbid curiosity. He watched as Delta squeezed her denim-clad ass and how…

"Can I buy you a drink?" a busty blonde asked as she sidled up to him, drawing his attention to her.

He was sure to keep his frown firmly in place as he locked eyes with her. "I'm good." He held up his beer.

Go away!

Her smile quickly died. Bay felt like a class-A dick as he watched her turn away; it couldn't be helped though. There was no point entertaining any advances. No point whatsoever.

"You turned that hottie down?" Beck asked as he hooked an arm around Bay's shoulders. "Are you crazy?"

"You are the one who's crazy. I shouldn't have let you talk me into this. It just reminds me of everything I can't have." He shoved Beck's arm away. He knew that the male meant well but some things were better left alone.

"You've been working ridiculous hours. You needed to blow off some steam."

"And how do you propose I do that?" He realized he was starting to sound like a sulking child. "Look, thank you for trying. I appreciate the sentiment but—"

"Why don't you just take the blonde home?" Beck raised his brows. "Have a little fun. Something is better than nothing."

"No." He shook his head. "Sometimes leaving things alone is for the best. No use flogging a dead horse."

"Horse?" Beck choked out a laugh. "Now you're exaggerating. I wouldn't call your dick a horse…"

Bay had to smile. He shook his head. "Thanks, bro, but no. You can stop now." He looked at the entrance to the bar. "I'm going to head out."

He could see that Beck wanted to argue.

"I'm tired. I'll take a walk, maybe have a swim – that's how I let off steam. Besides, it's getting late, I'm sure you'll be leaving soon."

Beck nodded. "Enjoy your swim."

Bay nodded back. "You enjoy your night."

His friend slapped him on the back. "I most certainly will."

He watched as the male headed back to the group of females he had been talking to, then Bay put down his beer and headed out.

He spotted her the instant his feet hit the pavement and stood there rooted to the spot.

Half an hour later…

The female wasn't human.

Not a chance. Bay took another swig of his beer, turning his gaze to the gyrating bodies on the dance floor. He had followed her into the bar across the street like an idiot. That question kept playing on his mind. *What was she?* It wasn't long before he was staring back at her, his eyes drawn to her lithe frame. She looked human enough, even though she was tall. Much taller than every other female in there. Tall and toned, wearing a tiny slip of a dress. No bra. Her breasts were the size of ripe peaches. Probably just as sweet. He ignored the voice in his head that made suggestions of sucking on them.

Stupid voice.

Stupid idea!

Instead, he kept his focus on her. She looked both nervous – her eyes kept darting about the room – *and* brimming with confidence – her chin had this tilt to it. A strange combination to be sure.

Bay took a few more steps towards her, trying hard not to openly scent the air. Finally, he found her scent in amongst all the warring smells. Not human. *Not a fuck!* Not with a scent like that. It was rich and very feminine with hints of flower nectar and notes of honey. Yet, it was distinctly masculine as well. *What the…!?* He'd never scented anything like it. How could someone scent of both a female and a male? It wasn't an overlapping masculine scent. It was coming *from* her. The essence of her. *Intriguing.*

He watched as yet another male approached her. Watched as she shot him down with a single shake of the head and a couple of well-directed words. Then she was leaning back, her ass against the bar, her gorgeous green eyes drifting across the room. Taking it all in, and yet not really focusing on anyone in particular. She toyed with a tumbler, holding it in one hand and then the other. Swirling her finger around the rim, finally clutching the glass against her chest. Not drinking any of the amber liquid inside. Not even a sip.

He had to know.

Had to.

Couldn't resist any longer. Bay ran a hand through his hair. He'd been told he was attractive. Not that it mattered. Then again, he found himself wanting to please her. Stupid but true. He prayed she didn't shoot him down like she had all the rest. Especially since he wasn't after what the other males wanted. Bay had to know *what* she was. Then he would be satisfied. Then he could go for that walk and take that swim. Get rid of some of this brimming energy. He didn't belong there. Should not have come in the first place. He felt a pang but quickly shoved it aside. He'd felt sorry for himself for far too many years. Bitterness and anger were his best friends for a while there. Those emotions didn't help anything though, so he didn't dwell much on them anymore.

Not much.

There was the odd occasion where it flared back up. Like in this moment, looking at this female made him feel everything all over again. He took a deep drink of his beer, pulled in a breath and headed over to her. The sooner this was done, the sooner he could leave.

Not all that long ago, he used to have confidence enough for three males. Those days were over. She looked up as he approached, looking indifferent. He'd even go so far as to say she looked bored. Then her eyes widened and her lips parted. Her nostrils flared and her eyes lit with interest. Not the rejection he'd been expecting then.

One of the most spectacular looking females he had ever seen, began her slow perusal of him, starting at his feet and working her way up. Her nostrils flared again as her startling green eyes met his. They were vivid, like newly unfurled leaves on a seedling. They glinted, her attention focused solely on him. *Well fuck!*

"Not human." She shook her head, narrowing her eyes in confusion. Her voice was silky and smooth, with a hint of smoke around the edges.

Bay had to smile. "I could say the same about you."

She nodded once, a smile toying with the edges of her lips. She didn't say anything more.

"So…" she began. He stepped in a little closer, not wanting those around them to eavesdrop. She raised her brows, looking him in the eye. Only marginally shorter than he was, Bay noted. She had a pair of legs on her that went on for miles. "Do you like what you see?" She finally smiled and holy shit but she was gorgeous. Several males stopped to openly stare.

He chuckled like a whelp before finally managing to stop himself. Just in time too. Any more of that type of behavior and he'd embarrass himself. Make it very clear to any watching that he didn't do this often…make that ever. "Yes." No use lying. "Very much so." He rubbed his chin, the light stubble catching against his hand. "I need to know one thing, and then I'll be out of your hair."

"Let me guess, what is a female like me doing in a place like this?" She must have caught the look in his eyes because she shook her head. "No! What about, did it hurt when you fell from heaven?"

Bay frowned. "What? No…I—"

She smiled, it was radiant. "One male asked me if I was a light switch. He wanted the opportunity to turn me on." She rolled her eyes.

Bay choked out a laugh. He hadn't heard anything so stupid in all his life. "Human males tried those pick-up lines on you?"

She nodded. "There are more if you want to hear?"

He shook his head. "That's okay. Did any of them actually work?"

She shook her head. "I'm still here. In fact, I was just about to head back to my hotel." She put the glass down on the bar. Then her eyes lifted in thought. "If you don't have a cheesy pick-up line, what did you want to ask me?"

Ceri hoped whatever it was, that it was good. She found herself feeling a little disappointed that it wasn't some cheesy pick-up line. This male was something. She wasn't sure what had possessed her to head out tonight. Sex with a human had seemed like a good idea after staring at the four walls of her hotel room but almost the moment she arrived there, she had changed her mind. They were puny, they tried too hard. None of them scented of anything remotely interesting. And now…he was there. This tall, dark, sexy specimen of a male. He scented like nothing she had savored before. Like chili and dark chocolate and smoke. Her mouth watered for a taste.

"I wanted to ask," he leaned in, speaking softly, "what are you? I scent..." He narrowed his eyes. "You look female, but I scent male as well. It makes no sense. The female scent is stronger," he frowned, like he was thinking it through, "quite delicious actually."

She laughed, watching as his cheeks turned a light shade of pink. This male was shy and sweet. Not just sexy as sin. Most of the males of her species were downright arrogant. There was a vulnerability to this male she found appealing. "Are you enquiring about my sex?" She narrowed her eyes at him. "Don't I look like a female?" She pretended to be put out.

His gaze dropped to her breasts and his cheeks reddened. His Adam's apple worked as he swallowed. Then his eyes widened and he sucked in a breath as they locked back with hers. "No, I mean, yes...you look feminine. You look really good." He squeezed his eyes shut and swiped his hand over his face. "I was just wondering what species you were...that's all."

This male was adorable. "What's your name?"

"Bay," he responded immediately. "And yours?"

"You must be a shifter," she blurted.

His jaw tightened and he shrugged. "Good guess since shifters are the most common of the non-humans. I'm certainly no elf." He touched one of his ears.

"Yeah, but which kind of shifter?"

"I didn't say I was a shifter. When did this become about me?" He raised his brows.

He hadn't denied it either. She didn't scent dog or bear or...it was puzzling. Maybe he wasn't a shifter. That couldn't be though. Like he had pointed out, he wasn't sporting elf ears – so, not an elf.

Most shifters knew the scent of a vampire when they smelled it. This male didn't. Ceri didn't think he ventured out often.

He leaned in again. So close that his breath tickled her ear when he spoke. "I'm a dragon." Her nipples tightened.

Ceri inhaled deeply, taking his scent in. "Of course you are." How had she missed that? The chili was fiery. The scent of smoke was very much at the fore. The dark chocolate made her mouth water for a taste.

He straightened up. "Your turn."

Disappointment rushed through her once again. This was the part where she told him and he high-tailed it out of there. Their species was not well loved. "I'm a vampire." She held her breath.

His whole frame tensed. Then he nodded. "You drink blood?" He frowned.

She smiled. "Yes, regularly. Although my last feed was two days ago – from my best friend, a male. That's who you scent on me."

His eyes lit with realization. "That makes sense."

"This is the part where you excuse yourself and run." Such a pity. He would make a good lover, she was sure.

"Is it?" He lifted his brows.

She pushed out a sigh. "Yes, humans and non-humans alike are either afraid of us or put off by our…food requirements."

He looked amused. "What is your name?"

"You can call me Carmine." Maybe this would go her way and if it did, she didn't want him knowing who she really was. He couldn't ever find her, or…*Hold on, Ceri! Calm yourself!* Nothing had happened. Nothing might happen. She was getting ahead of herself. One thing was for sure though, she did want him. Very badly.

He quirked a brow. "I can call you Carmine. I take it that's not your real name?"

She shrugged. "We don't need names, do we?"

He shrugged. "I guess not. I am neither afraid nor put off." He put out his hand and she took it. Strong, firm...and very warm. They shook. "It's good to meet you."

"You too." She smiled. "I was just headed back to my hotel. It's a block or two up the road. Would you like to walk me back?" Normally she wouldn't dance around something quite this much. If she wanted to rut someone she came right out and said it, but she had a feeling she might spook this one. This, despite him being handsome. He oozed confidence, but at the same time there was a shy edge to him. She would even go so far as to say that he was a little awkward. Ceri found that she liked the combination. Liked it a lot.

"Yeah, sure." He put his beer down on the bar. "I was about to leave anyway."

She walked ahead of him, feeling his eyes on her. The air was crisp. Ceri sucked in a deep breath as they walked outside. "I'm a couple of blocks up the road." She pointed to the five-story building not far up ahead. "You take the next right and it's about a block down."

"Ocean view." He raised his brows.

"Yes, it's right on the beach." She nodded.

"Nice." He smiled and they began to walk.

"What brings you to Beachhaven?" The male frowned. "It's a little far from your neck of the woods...Sweetwater, right?"

She nodded. "Very good, you know a little about us."

"A little." He nodded. "So, what brings you here?"

"Even vampires need a vacation."

His smile widened.

"I love the ocean. Love lazing around on the beach in my bikini. I love swimming. My absolute favorite," she raised her brows, "don't laugh."

He shook his head. "Never. Why would I laugh? There's nothing wrong with downtime."

"I love snorkeling as well." She licked her lips. "I discovered it a few years ago. Now I take a beach holiday every chance I can get. I know," she rolled her eyes, "a vampire who loves to swim and snorkel." She made a face. "It's especially laughable considering the myth that we turn to ashes in the sun." She pushed out a nervous-sounding laugh, realizing that she *was* nervous. Very much so.

Bay shrugged. "I think it's great. I happen to be a Water dragon. We have a natural affinity with water, especially with the ocean."

She frowned. "A Water dragon. Forgive me, I don't know much about your kind."

"That's because we don't get out much." He grinned. *So cute!* He wore a black button-down shirt, top two buttons open, a pair of dark jeans. His blue eyes glinted in the streetlight.

"You don't." She shook her head. "You're the first dragon I've ever met."

"You're the first vampire I have met, so I guess that makes us even."

She nodded. They arrived at the entrance to her hotel. "I would love to hear more about…Water dragons…your species in general. Can I entice you up for a drink?"

He seemed hesitant. *Why?* By the way he'd looked at

her earlier, she could tell that he was interested. He'd openly admitted to liking what he saw when she'd asked him, and yet...he was still hesitating. "It's just a drink. I won't bite or anything." She laughed at her stupid joke, wishing she hadn't made it. Especially considering how he barely smiled.

"Yeah, why not." He finally shrugged. "One drink and then I must go."

His lack of enthusiasm both irritated and excited her. Ceri was used to getting males she wanted. Never for anything other than a rut though. She was not able to bear children, so male vampires tended to steer clear of anything that smacked of commitment. Not that she'd actually met anyone she wanted to spend any real time with. *Please!* She used her keycard to gain access to the building and made her way to the elevator.

The shifter followed close on her heels. She pushed the button for the fifth and highest floor. "You said you don't get out much. Is that the case for dragon shifters in general, or specifically you?"

"Both."

Cryptic.

The elevator dinged as they reached her floor. The door opened. Ceri put her hand on the edge of the door as it opened. "Both? As in...?" She raised her brows, moving into the door of the elevator and essentially closing him in.

"Dragon shifters are only permitted to...mingle with humans twice per year."

"Otherwise you're homebound?"

"Yes." He nodded, stepping towards the exit. Towards her. His scent was incredible.

"Why do your males mingle with humans?" It seemed

an odd thing to do. She could guess but hearing it from him would be way more fun.

"We have very few female dragons." He shrugged.

"So 'mingle' is not the right word?" She smiled to show she was only teasing.

Another one-shouldered shrug. His eyes glinted with mischief. More of his scent enveloped her. Drool-worthy. She swallowed down her need to drink from him. Her gums itched. She'd eaten just two short days before. She didn't need blood. Not so soon. She wanted it though. Wanted *his* blood.

"You said you don't get out much and that it's not only because you're a dragon shifter. There's more to it then?"

"I haven't been into town for a couple of years now. Single males go on the Stag Runs religiously."

"Stag Runs?" She laughed. "I guess it's a good name. Why don't you go on them?" She knew she was prying. If he had wanted to tell her, he would have. Then another thought occurred to her. "You're single, aren't you?"

"Yes, very much so. The Stag Run is not my thing. Males come into towns like this one to rut and…" He let the sentence die.

"You don't like rutting?" She frowned.

Bay smiled, he had this strange look about him. His eyes seemed clouded. His demeanor, down somehow. "Don't answer that." She put up her hand. "It's none of my business," she laughed, trying to shove aside the heaviness that suddenly filled the space.

She waited for him to say something. To answer her or to change the subject… something, but he just looked uncomfortable. Ceri stepped out of the elevator and into the hallway.

She didn't have to walk far. "This is mine." She stopped

at the first door, using the keycard to open it. "Come on in." She pushed the door open and leaned against the jamb, allowing him plenty of space to enter in front of her.

His eyes locked with hers. They heated. He was definitely interested, so why was he acting like being there was the worst idea? More importantly, why did that intrigue her so much?

CHAPTER 2

What the fuck was he doing there?
      What was the point?

To chat. There was no way this stunning, beguiling, utterly sensual creature only wanted him there so that they could chat. A human? Maybe. A Vampire? Forget about it. He didn't know much about the species, just that non-humans saw things differently.

Bay didn't feel like chatting much himself. In fact, the more he thought about what he wanted, the more upset he felt. He wanted to give this female pleasure, wanted to see the expression on her face as she let go. Wanted to see her beautiful green eyes hazy with passion.

He could scent her interest in him. Could see it. Pity, she was barking up the wrong tree. He should just wish her a good night and leave. Except his feet carried him further and further into the hotel room.

Bay swallowed thickly as his eyes landed on the bed. The room was spacious with a desk and chair, as well as a lounge area, but all he could see was the damned bed. He really should leave. "Take a seat." Carmine walked in beside him and gestured to a sofa. "The minibar has a nice selection, unless you would prefer a tea, coffee…soda maybe?" He watched as the column of her neck moved.

She was nervous. A female like Carmine should not be nervous. She was sure to get plenty of offers and on a daily basis. Then again, he'd seen it with his own eyes. Those human males had been falling over their feet just to get near her. Non-humans would be no different. Just look at him as an example. He really shouldn't be there and yet he couldn't help himself.

He did as she said, choosing the single wingback chair. Why was he torturing himself? Torturing them both? "I'll have a whiskey. Neat."

She nodded once, taking two tumblers from the cupboard. Then she leaned right over, ass in the air, as she opened the small fridge. Her long legs unveiling even more as her dress pulled up, all the way up.

Holy fuck.

Giving him a spectacular visual of her pussy. Pink and oh so fucking pretty. Bay put his hand between his legs and gave his cock a squeeze. He didn't know what he had expected to find. In truth, if a female was going to bring life back to his shaft. This was certainly the one to have done it. But there was nothing. Not a stirring. Not a rumbling. Only a familiar hunger, deep down inside. Did he enjoy rutting? Yes. Did he want to rut? Abso-fucking-lutely. Could he do it? Did he have the physical capability? No, that basic function was taken away from him years ago. Whether he deserved it or not was a debate he had with himself on a regular basis. It wasn't important right then though. Bay shuffled in his seat, trying to get comfortable. Trying to quell the raging need that coursed through him.

Carmine straightened up and air could fill his lungs once more. He pushed out a heavy breath. She uncapped the tiny bottles and poured them into the tumblers.

Whiskey for the both of them. Then she sauntered to Bay in three easy steps and handed him one of the glasses. Their eyes locked. The need in hers was apparent, he was sure it would match his own. Her delicious scent wrapped itself around him. Funnily enough, the masculine scent was all but gone. It hadn't really bugged him, but she scented way better right then. Too damned good.

Bay tipped the glass in her direction and then downed the contents. The whiskey burned its way down his throat.

She raised her brows in question but did the same, licking her lips and placing the glass on the table.

"So, we've had our drinks," Bay said. He should leave. He didn't want to.

"Are you going to leave now?" She could obviously sense his hesitancy.

"No," he fingered the hem of her dress. "I'd like to stay a little longer and I think it's time we cut to the chase."

"Agreed." Her eyes were bright with excitement. Pity she was going to be disappointed in the end. Disappointed in one way maybe, but he'd leave her very well sated. That much was for sure.

"Do you want me to make you come?" Bay just out and said it. Screw all this dancing around.

She laughed, tilting her head back slightly. Even that was as sexy as fuck. "Most males would have used the word fuck or rut. I like you, dragon, and yes, I would like it very much if you would make me come. I would've been more upfront from the start, but I got the distinct impression that you would have run a mile."

Bay couldn't smile back. Disappointment ate at him. The female was right. He should have run, should run now but he couldn't. He needed this, even if no physical pleasure could be derived from this for himself. He wanted the vampire to have pleasure. He would at least enjoy giving it to her. Bay nodded. "I'll make you come. More than once if you would like, but it needs to be on my terms."

Her eyes widened and she pushed out a breath, clearly startled. Then the one side of her mouth quirked up. "You have got to be the most interesting male I have ever met. Most would have had me on all fours already."

He had to hold back a cringe. Given the opportunity, she would have been on her knees. He felt arousal deep in his belly. Felt a zing of need but there was no rush of blood to his groin. No erection. "Here's the deal." He leaned back in the chair so that he could take her in. "*I give you pleasure. I touch you.*"

She frowned. "So, I don't get to touch you back? Is that what you're saying?"

"You get to feel."

"I think I might enjoy touching you though—"

He shook his head. He didn't want this beautiful vampire to know his greatest shame. To see pity instead of need written in her eyes would fuck him up. "I touch you. That's the deal. Otherwise, I walk out."

She licked her lips. "Can we kiss?"

He shrugged. "If I kiss you, then yes, you can kiss me back."

"What if I want to suck your dick? Or ride you?"

Bay had to squeeze his eyes shut at the images that accosted him. His damned cock remained just as flaccid as ever. This was such a bad idea. Bay shook his head. "No! Take off your dress and lie on that bed." He pointed at the king-size. "You can touch yourself, or clutch the bedsheets, I don't care either way. The only thing I want you to do is come. Can you do that, Carmine?"

She nodded once and cleared her throat. "I think I can do that." Then she took a step back and peeled the dress from her body, pulling it over her head.

Bay drank her in. He didn't need a working cock to know she was sexy. Didn't need one to know that he wanted her with every fiber of his being. "You are beautiful," he murmured. Her breasts were pink-tipped. Ripe peaches indeed. Not too big and not too small. Utterly breathtaking. Her skin was like porcelain. The scent of her arousal made his mouth water. Nectar and honey. She turned, giving him a fantastic view of her ass. Two globes of perfection. Tight and spank-worthy. Not that he was into that kind of kinky shit, but a female like this could convert the fucking dead.

Well almost.

She lay down on the bed, her throat working. She chewed on her lower lip, eyes on the ceiling.

He was going to make the most of this. The most of her. "Open your legs." His voice was a rough rasp. It wasn't like he did this sort of thing anymore. Not like he would do it again any time soon.

Her breathing hitched and the edge of her mouth turned up, just a fraction. "Are you always this bossy?"

"Only when it counts."

She smiled and did as he said, sliding her legs open, revealing utter perfection. Soft pink folds, already glistening with her need. Carmine planted her feet on the comforter. Her chest heaved.

"You're already turned on and I haven't even touched you yet." A fact.

The vampire nodded. "We're receptive and a highly sexual species. I haven't had sex in a good couple of weeks."

"Weeks." Bay snorted out a laugh. Then he put up a hand. "I'm sorry." He didn't want her asking questions. Didn't want her to know how long it had been for him.

"So you—" she began. Her eyes flared and she made a soft yelping noise as he closed the space between them and pushed his tongue into her channel. Deep inside.

Fuck!

By scale and claw, she tasted better than she scented. So damned sweet. Carmine made a keening noise and grabbed at the comforter. There was a ripping sound as her nails tore through the material. She moaned as he tongue-fucked her. All out groaned as he moved to her clit. It was plump as fuck. Fit in his mouth, against his tongue perfectly. Bay licked and sucked, alternating between the two. He'd let her come quickly this time. Just this time, though.

By the sounds she was making, he knew she was close. Bay suckled her, simultaneously rubbing his tongue across her nub. Her legs closed around his head and her back bowed. She was strong, her grip tight. Not like humans. Delicate and weak. This was something different. He found himself intrigued and watched as she threw her head back and groaned. Long and deep until she finally slumped back, she was breathing heavily. "Oh. My. God!" She sucked in more air, like she couldn't get enough. "That was so good."

Actually, he was rusty. The next one would be better.

She lifted her head. Her long hair was tussled. Her green eyes, cat-like eyes, were bright. Glowing slightly. She smiled, almost lazily. He was shocked to see fangs. By fire, but they were long and sharp as fuck. Sexy as anything.

"I'm sorry." She touched a finger to her lips. "This is normal for a vampire. I'm just really turned on and—"

"No need to explain." He shook his head.

"You're okay with it? With me?"

"More than okay." It shocked him that she was so self-conscious. Her. This ravishing creature.

She nodded. "Thank you." She cast her gaze down. "I guess we're so used to being called names. Things like bloodsuckers and monsters. We're called filthy and—"

"I don't see you as any of those things."

"Undress." Her eyes tracked down his torso.

Bay gave a single shake of the head. *If only! If fucking only.*

She wanted him. Ceri wanted him so badly. She wanted his cock deep inside her. Wanted her fangs deep inside him. Somehow, she just knew he wouldn't mind if she drank from him. She'd never been with anyone other than a vampire. Drinking and fucking went hand-in-hand. She wasn't sure she could do one without the other. "I want you inside me," she moaned.

Bay nodded once. He kneeled between her parted thighs, taking her in with his eyes. Ceri had to stop herself from squirming under his scrutiny. She had never had a male look at her with that degree of hunger. Of pure unadulterated need. It was feral and almost unnerving. It was also arousing. She dug her hands into the already destroyed comforter, trying to stop herself from reaching out and touching him. His shirt pulled tight on his well-muscled frame. She wanted to rip it from his body. Wanted to feast, not only with her fangs but with her eyes as well. He was magnificent. From his blue eyes – they had this silvery edge to them – to his masculine jaw. His lips were made for kissing.

He leaned over her, not actually touching her. His eyes

burned into hers as his lips sought hers. Hungry and demanding from the start. She couldn't close her eyes. Couldn't stop looking into the depths of his. Then his fingers were breaching her pussy.

By blood. By all that was red. The air caught in her lungs as he found her spot. Found it immediately and went to work on it. Her eyes widened in both shock and pleasure. She broke the kiss as her fangs lengthened all over again. Her throat felt dry but there was no time to think about it.

Extreme pleasure. It rushed through her. She realized with a start that she had wrapped her legs around his hips. He hovered above her. His whole body remained poised. For a second she thought he might stop. She unlocked her legs, planting her feet in the comforter. It wasn't like she could move much since his hand held her in place. Fingers still pumping. Slowly. The tips brushing against her g-spot. She groaned so deeply, it almost came out sounding like a growl.

His thumb brushed against her clit. Once. Twice. Then nothing but the slow, lazy brush of his fingers. Deep inside her. The slick sounds her body was making filled the room.

"Feels good," she pushed out between pants.

Bay leaned in, he kissed her neck. He nipped her softly. A zing of need raced through her. The need to come. The need to bite and be bitten. Her fangs lengthened even more. It would be amazing if he bit her. Really bit her. Too much to hope for or to ask for. He nipped her again and her pussy clenched around his fingers. Bay stopped moving, circling her clit with his thumb instead. She arched her back.

"I want you," she choked out, having to grip the

comforter to keep herself from cupping his jaw. From running her hands down his chest. She wanted to cup his balls. Wanted to feel the hard length of him in her hands…inside her.

"I want you too." It came out sounding choked and desperate. His eyes were narrowed and clouded. Filled with need. His jaw was tight.

He began to pump his fingers again. Just the right combination of hard and deep. Yet, soft and careful. His thumb found her clit and rubbed. The strokes both soft and firm.

Good lord! No male had touched her like this. He knew where and just how to do it. There was that familiar coiling sensation in the pit of her stomach. Her eyes were wide and her breathing ragged.

The dragon looked down at her with such an intense look in his eyes. It was clear he wanted to watch her come. The realization turned her on even more. Vampire males normally put her on her knees and took what they needed. Her orgasm was a byproduct of that. Any foreplay was normally to get her wet enough for penetration. They would drink from her at their climax, ensuring she finished as well. It was almost clinical. A means to an end. This was different. This was intense. Unreal. That look of longing in his eyes. The way he watched. The coiling intensified. Her body began to tense, preparing for release.

Her cries grew louder. Her fangs felt impossibly long, her mouth impossibly dry. Her legs were around his hips again, but she couldn't bring herself to move them this time.

Then she was falling, a cry torn from her as her head rocked back. Her eyes felt like they had rolled to the back of her skull. His fingers kept working their magic. It felt like he was touching her everywhere. Her body tensed. There was a ripping noise as pleasure flooded her.

Without thinking – how could she in a moment like this – she leaned forward, sinking her fangs into his flesh. Whether his neck, his arm, his chest, she wasn't sure.

Rapture. Delicious rapture hit her tongue as her orgasm intensified, her muscles pulling impossibly tight as she sucked in another gulp of hot, rich blood. Dark chocolate, chili all wrapped in a delicious smokiness. Never had she tasted a better combination.

This mouthful burned on the way down. Heating her and heating and heating and—*By fang!* Ceri pulled back, her mouth on fire. Her whole body burning up from the inside out. The air froze in her lungs with the intensity. His silvery-blue eyes held hers. It hurt, but it felt good too. She was dumbstruck for a few moments. Energy coursed through her. Her chest heaved and she felt that her mouth was hanging open. Ceri couldn't close it. Couldn't move. She felt a drop of his blood drip down from the edge of her mouth. It burned a path down the side of her cheek. She half expected to see smoke coil up. Pain and intense pleasure all rolled into one. Delicious and agonizing.

His fingers stopped moving mid-pump. A frown appeared, creasing his brow. His eyes filled with…shock. Then they widened with surprise. Smoke curled from his nostrils. So damned sexy. She felt his blood inside her. Potent. Deadly and yet beautiful somehow. Just like the male himself.

Was he upset that she had taken from him?

She wanted to apologize, but her mouth wouldn't work. Her orgasm had left her spent. His blood had left her dumb…reeling…yet oddly, still aroused. It had physically hurt to drink from him – even such a small amount – but she wanted more.

"Fuck," Bay choked out. "What the—?" More frowning. He looked down and then back at her and then he threw his head back and roared. His big chest heaved. More smoke billowed from his nose, his mouth. One of the most terrifying and yet utterly beautiful things she had ever seen. Bay ripped at his pants and lunged at her, almost at the same time.

Part of her wanted to run or to take up a defensive position. Her eyes may even have flashed red but it didn't deter him. The rest of her filled with excitement like she'd never felt before. He grabbed her thighs, his touch harsh and rushed. There was a strange look of confusion and desire on his face. It made her heart race and her pussy clench with need. Like the last two orgasms had never happened.

CHAPTER 3

His cock was hard.
Hard.

He was erect. Fully erect. His dick throbbing. His balls full and tight. Need coiling in his belly. He could scent her pussy, could still taste her on his tongue. How long would this last? A minute? An hour?

He needed to be inside her and right fucking then. Urgency and bewilderment rushed through him as he tore at his pants. His jeans came apart with a loud rip. His erect cock sprang free.

Hold up! The vampire had fear in her eyes. He needed to try to calm down. More smoke billowed from his nose and mouth. Right then he was glad he wasn't a Fire dragon. He might actually hurt her with his urgency and need. Might burn down this whole damned hotel. He didn't have very much control. Felt his scales rub, was quite sure some of his dragon would be at the fore. Enough for her to see. She might be frightened, but she was also aroused. She made no move to leave. To stop him. The fear was mingled with arousal and interest. Thank fuck because he doubted he could stop. He had to be inside her and right fucking then.

He grabbed her thighs, hoisting them up and around

him and slid inside her in one hard thrust. Another roar was pulled from him as he felt her pussy tight, soft velvety…so hot. So wet. Her mouth dropped open and her eyes heated some more. He squeezed his eyes shut, a pained grunting noise escaped him.

Bay didn't think he'd ever be able to feel this again. "Fuck!" he groaned as he ground into her welcoming flesh. Him hard and her so damned soft. Blood rushed to his head. He could hear his heart beating. Could hear the blood running through his veins. He groaned *fuck,* each time he pushed into her. The female whimpered. He could only hope it was pleasure she was feeling. Thankfully she wasn't human, he might damage her if she were. His control was slipping and fast. Couldn't stop himself. Couldn't think. Could only feel.

Ten seconds later and his balls exploded. He was glad shifters couldn't die easily, because he was sure he would've died just then had that been the case. From a heart attack, a stroke, or possibly both at once. He growled so long and hard it felt like his throat was rubbed raw. Seed erupted from him in hot spurts. His eyes were open and yet he didn't see anything except for maybe bright white stars.

He couldn't stop moving. Kept rocking into her. Surprise flooded him all over again as he realized his cock was still hard. He stifled a laugh, looking down at the vampire who was looking at him with amusement. The sides of her mouth quirked up in the start of a smile. Her eyes glinted as well.

Oh fuck! He'd forgotten about the female. Had only thought of his own need. Not that anyone could blame him.

He'd make her come this time. It had been a very long

time since he'd been inside a female, but he was sure he could still remember how it was done. Properly that is.

His chest was plastered against hers. His nose barely an inch away from hers.

"I don't think I've seen anyone enjoy a rut as much as that." She smiled, a little out of breath. "You look shocked. Like that was your first time or something." She frowned, narrowing her eyes in on his.

"No, not my first time." He was still panting heavily. His body vibrating. "It has been a while though." The last thing Bay felt like doing was talking. He hadn't come there to talk. She hadn't invited him there for that purpose.

Sweat dripped from his brow as he lifted her legs over his shoulders. Not only beautiful and receptive as fuck, she was also flexible. He squeezed his eyes shut, gritting his teeth as he pulled back. So amazing. He growled low in his throat as he sank back into her. Carmine groaned softly as well. Bay fucked her using hard even strokes. He. Fucked. Her.

Fucked.

He was rutting.

How was this possible? He didn't care. Not right then. Later they could talk. Right then he was going to partake and give. Both in equal measure. He leaned down so that her knees were on either side of her head. Her pelvis tilted forward, giving him deeper access. He groaned as he took full advantage. Her eyes widened and her mouth dropped open as she sucked in a ragged breath.

He'd hoped to take it a little slower this time but his body had other ideas, he couldn't stop the need coursing through him. The need to thrust and to come and to do it again and again.

"Fuck!" he ground out. Couldn't seem to say anything

else – or think it, for that matter.

Fuck.

Fuck.

Fuck.

That was it. He slipped a hand between them and sought her tight bundle of nerves, strumming it in even strokes. Trying to go easy and failing. She clenched her teeth, her eyes rolling back as her pussy clamped down on him. She whimpered and then groaned deeply as her body came around him. The sound, the feeling of her tight channel, the slapping noises his balls made against her—

"Fuuuuuuck!" Bay yelled as his second orgasm squeezed his balls even tighter than the first. It was more powerful but ended quicker. That was until he felt a stinging sensation. He watched in fascination as she sank her fangs into the inside of his wrist and then sucked.

Bay felt the tug on his arm right through to his dick. Like a livewire was connecting one to the other. Another orgasm rocked him. It was powerful. Mind-blowing. His body crouched over her. He clamped his other hand on her leg to hold her in place. His hips jerked forward. She sucked a second time. More intense pleasure, almost to the point of pain. Then she released him, turning her face away, whimpering as her pussy continued to pulse and spasm. *Fuuuuck!* Wave after wave of pleasure. His eyes were wide. His movements jerky. More smoke coiled from his nose until he was finally able to slow his movements.

"More," he groaned. "Please." He wasn't beyond begging.

She turned her face back to him, her eyes hazy, her lids at half-mast. He almost yelled with sheer joy when she nodded once, licking her lips.

He pulled out of her with a loud grunt, flipping her

onto her knees. Carmine sank down onto her elbows, pushing her ass up. Seed dripped down her inner thighs. His seed. Then a sobering thought hit. "Oh fuck!" he growled. "I didn't use protection. Are you…is this—" He could hear the panic in his voice. He'd never even considered becoming a father. It wasn't something he'd thought about in a long time because it shouldn't have been possible.

"Relax dragon." She looked back at him. Her eyes clouded with sorrow. She shook her head slowly. "I am unable to have young. Not only are my hips too narrow but I went under a silver knife many years ago making it an impossibility."

"Silver knife? What knife? Why would you—?"

She sat up, clasping her hands in her lap. "Many of our females died trying to birth young. They, like myself, had pelvises that were too narrow to birth a child." She sat on her haunches. She looked down. Her hips were indeed narrow. "As you must know, having a C-section, like a human, is not possible with our healing capabilities. Up until recently, females with my condition were sterilized."

"That's barbaric!"

"Yes, but it still remains the safest thing to do. Like I said, we are highly sexual creatures, unable to refrain from sex. Once we become pregnant, it is pretty much a death sentence. Nowadays, some females opt to take birth control but it is not always effective. We still lose a female on occasion. It is a risk some are willing to take."

"Why would they take the chance?" He thought about his own predicament. "I guess I understand. Sometimes death isn't the worst thing."

"It seems we are compatible with shifters – wolves and bears, that is – I'm not sure about your kind. The length of the pregnancy is much shorter and the young are very small. Small enough to pass safely through the pelvis. We only learned of this in recent years."

"Why didn't you choose birth control? Surely it would have been better?"

"I am an older vampire. Not that I'm old," she quickly added. "But old enough to have missed out on being given an option."

"That is sad. I am sorry." He meant it wholeheartedly.

"It's okay, I have learned to live with it." He saw pain in her eyes. "The option was not afforded to me." She shook her head sadly. "There was only one route back then and that was surgery." Her eyes clouded and her shoulders slumped. "I am upset about it at times." She looked away. "My womb was cut from my body with a silver knife. It grew back but for some reason when cut away with silver, the organ is no longer functional."

Holy crap!

Just like him. His heart beat faster. He felt sorry for her. Knew what she was feeling.

"Don't look at me like that." She shook her head.

"Like what?"

"Like you pity me." She crawled over to him and straddled him, her hands on his shoulders.

"I do, but it's not what you think." This was pity born of understanding.

The vampire smiled. "Can I touch you yet?" Her smile widened and she tightened her hold on his shoulders.

Bay chuckled. His dick jutted hard and proud from his body. Her eyes were on it, feasting. "Yes, you may touch me…anywhere, as much as you want."

"Good." There was the sound of fabric tearing and buttons went flying.

Bay laughed as he shrugged the ruined shirt from his body. He'd forgotten he was even wearing it. He still had his shoes on, still wore his broken jeans. He didn't care. Not about his state of dress or anything else for that matter. The vampire was sinking onto his cock. Her tight pussy wrapping around him. He grabbed her hips, holding her in place, watching her breasts bounce softly as she rode him. She was beautiful to behold. This felt like a gift. His hands tightened on her as he became lost in the moment.

Bay sprang up, throwing the tattered covers from the bed. She was gone. He knew it like he knew his own name. The fact didn't stop him from checking anyway. From searching the room, as well as the adjoining bathroom. From pulling open the closet and cursing when he found it empty.

The vampire was gone. The sun wasn't up yet. His internal clock told him it would be soon but not yet. She'd up and left before he could talk to her. Find out how this was possible. If it would happen again.

He looked down at his flaccid cock. It was hardly surprising. They'd fucked many, many times. So many times his balls actually ached. He felt weak and tired and in the best possible way. She had bitten him several times. The marks were already gone. Healed up. If it weren't for his achy body and the fact that he was in a strange hotel room, he would never say any of it had happened.

But it had.

The vampire was real.

Only he didn't know her real name or where to find her. He couldn't exactly walk into her coven. He knew she wouldn't want that, knew she would turn him away. Would be angry with him even. Dragons and vampires didn't mix.

He was a leader now. In charge of the Water Warriors. His king was counting on him to lead effectively. Flying into vampire territory was not the way to go about things. Demanding to speak to a nameless female. *No!* He couldn't do it.

Bay picked up the phone next to the bed and pushed the button that had 'Reception' written under it. Two rings later and a male answered.

What the hell did he say? "I'm calling from room…" He read the number on the phone, "516 – I was wondering where the female went. The one who—"

"Oh, yes, Miss Carmine. She checked out. Said you…um…Mr Bay, is that correct?"

"Yes, it is," he said, feeling disappointment so acute it had him almost reeling. Bay sat down on the bed, landing hard.

He had to work to actually comprehend what the male was saying. "She said you might want to stay in the room. You would be most welcome. All charges for her account. She mentioned an accident with the comforter."

Bay looked down at the bed. The comforter was on the floor and ripped to shreds. So were the sheets, and the mattress was a mess as well.

"The sheets might—"

"It's all to be charged to Miss Carmine's account. The room is fully paid for until 10 am on Tuesday morning."

"Did Miss Carmine leave a note or her contact details?"

"No note and I'm afraid we can't give out any personal information."

"I understand."

"We hope you enjoy your stay, Mr Bay." His tone was upbeat.

"Thank you." He held the receiver to his ear even though he heard a click telling him the other male was off the line.

He finally allowed it to land on the cradle. Bay scrubbed a hand over his face and puffed out a breath. Why hadn't he asked the vampire for more information when he had the chance?

Like, how? How had taking his blood brought life back to his body? Would the effect be lasting? It was too soon to tell. He didn't want to know right then. Was too afraid of what the outcome would be.

He looked down at himself, cringing. There was no way he could leave this room looking like this, which meant one thing.

CHAPTER 4

"You have got to be shitting me?" Beck's eyes were wide. "Completely shitting me! I mean I can scent you rutted, so I know you aren't talking through your ass, but ..." He walked around the room. "I can scent it in here." He choked out a laugh. "Definitely on that bed which looks like it went to war. Go you!" He did a fist pump. "I can scent female all over you...you didn't hold back, by the way, did you?" The male chuckled, infuriating him.

"Stop!" Bay shook his head. "This is no laughing matter."

"What are you talking about? It's a great reason for celebration." Beck grinned. "You fucked a female." He made a yowling noise. "Went all out on her. I can tell." He sniffed the air. "Hey, I would have too if I'd been celibate for...how many years has it been again?"

"I didn't ask you to come here so that you could goad—"

"Come on!" Beck all but yelled. "You look like someone died. You should be celebrating. You're not impotent."

"I could still be. We don't know whether she cured me or not."

"Even if you are, at least you figured out something that gets things to work, right?"

"No, I haven't. Having sex with a vampire is not a solution." Bay shook his head. "You know how crazy that sounds, right? I can't just walk into a coven and announce myself. What would I say? Don't mind me, I'm here for a quick hook-up." *With one certain female. I'll take the one with the big green eyes, please.* He gave a quick shake of the head to banish the thought. It was plain stupid!

"Well, I guess you couldn't just walk in, but—"

"There are no buts! It can't happen. End of story!"

"You might be cured though. You haven't tested it out." Beck glanced down, in the general direction of his cock, making Bay want to cover himself up, especially considering he was only wearing a towel around his hips.

"I rutted a multitude of times, I doubt," Bay shook his head, "I'd have much luck if I tried now," he mumbled the last.

Beck made a face. "What are you talking about? You're a shifter. A dragon at that. If I can go all night and still wake up for a last round, so can you."

"I don't want to try right now. I'll—"

"Bullshit! You need to know. No use putting it off. Maybe you don't need a vampire female. Maybe you're cured. How amazing would that be?"

"I doubt it!" *It couldn't be that simple, could it?*

"Don't be so negative. You never know until you try." Beck pushed a bag into Bay's hands. "I bought the biggest sizes they had but I'm sure it's still going to be a bit tight."

Bay took the bag and mumbled his thanks.

"Now, go in there and make sure you test the equipment before you come back out." He pointed at the bathroom door.

Bay held the other male's stare for a few seconds before nodding. Beck was right. He went in, closing and locking the door behind him.

He heard Beck chuckle. "I won't come in or anything. It's not like I want to watch you whack off." He laughed some more. *Jackass!*

Bay wouldn't put it past the male. Beck being a bit of an asshole and all. The male had been there for him on many occasions though. Heck, he'd rutted enough for the both of them. Bay couldn't help but smile. His humor quickly evaporated when he removed the towel and starred down at his dick.

Shit! He didn't want to know. *No! He did.* Then again, he would find out soon enough, wouldn't he? Bay looked at the closed door. Beck would give him hell if he walked out of there without an answer. The male was right. He needed to bite the bullet, so to speak, and find out.

Bay spotted a small bottle of hotel lotion on the counter. He poured a generous amount onto his palm and rubbed the lotion onto his member.

Bay fisted his cock. He paused for a moment, considering not going through with it all over again. *Fuck it!* He had to know. With a sigh, he began to work his dick using slow, easy strokes.

He closed his eyes and pictured the vampire. So damned sexy. Bay stroked a little quicker. He'd taken her in a multitude of different positions. With her tight as fuck ass in the air. Watching her ride him was certainly something to behold. Her breasts could not be considered big, but they still jiggled and bounced each time she sat on his cock. Her pink nipples tight. Her moans like music to his ears. Her pussy had been tight and the prettiest pink. She—

Bay looked down. There was a tightness in his belly. Need coursing through his veins. He knew the feeling well. His dick was no longer completely flaccid but it was a long way from being hard. He knew if he carried on, it would bring him nothing but frustration. Somehow, he had known this would be the case. He'd known. How had it been possible with the vampire? Would it be possible with any vampire or just her? Frustration and disappointment ate at him.

He washed his hands, brushed his teeth and then hurriedly dressed into the undersized garments. Thankfully, he'd showered earlier. The jeans fit him around his waist but fell to well above his ankles. The t-shirt was snug around his chest and biceps. Bay didn't give a shit. It wasn't important.

He pulled in a deep breath and walked out into the other room. Beck jumped up off the sofa, his brows raised, a look of expectation on his face.

Bay shook his head and watched it turn to one of pity.

CHAPTER 5

One month later…

"You need to be sure to take these every day." Ceri handed the medication to the female.

Chantel nodded and took the box. "I will."

"You can't forget, not even once."

Chantel swallowed thickly, her eyes wide. "I know."

"You are now sexually active. If you forget to take your birth control, if you skip even one pill, then you will need to use condoms…human coverings. Here…" She dug in her drawer, taking out two boxes.

Chantel smiled. "I have a ton of those things at home. And a couple in my purse." She rooted around in the leather bag, pulling out a strip of condoms. "See?"

"You can never have enough," Ceri warned. "Abstinence is the best prevention…" Ceri saw the look on the other woman's face. "If you are unable to do that then you need to be careful. Ideally, double up on contraceptives."

"The males don't like it when you insist they wear a condom."

"Tough shit!" Ceri felt her blood boil. "They don't have to deal with the consequences. Trust me, if they want to rut, they'll be willing to do what it takes."

Chantel nodded. "You're right."

"Of course I am." Ceri pushed out a breath. She reached out and took the other female's arm. "I've seen females die. I've been there and felt helpless to stop it. Out of the seven females, we only managed to save one. Her baby died in the end, they all did." She felt a lump rise in her throat.

Chantel nodded, looking shell-shocked.

"I'm not telling you this to shock you…okay, maybe I am and to scare you a little. You have to remember to take your birth control every day, and you can't let these males bully you. Your life is at stake here. Either you refrain, or you be responsible, there is no other option."

"There is one." Chantel held up a finger and cocked her head. "I could have the surgery."

"You would need to think long and hard before going that route. It isn't reversible." Ceri felt her chest tighten. "You are too young to be contemplating something so life-changing."

"Did you have the surgery? I heard somewhere in passing that you had."

Ceri was just on the cusp age-wise. Some females were clearly old enough to have definitely gone under the knife while others were far too young. Ceri was at that questionable age. The coven was big, but not big enough. Everyone was in everyone else's business. It was at times like this that she was acutely aware of that fact. She nodded. "Yes, I had the surgery and I'm going to urge you to think carefully before doing something so drastic."

"Do you regret it?"

"I didn't have a choice so," she shrugged, "there is nothing to regret."

"Yeah, but do you wish things could be different?"

Ceri pushed out a breath. It was hard talking about this. The last time she had, she'd been with the dragon shifter. What a night that had been. Again, not something to think on right then. She nodded. "I do regret it. I would give anything to be able to go back and change things. You are lucky you have a choice."

"I do have a choice but like you said, having sex is risky." She shrugged. "Maybe I should consider—"

"No!" Ceri held up a hand. "You are far too young to even consider it. You would never be able to have young. Never ever, can you comprehend that?"

"I couldn't have young now, so what's the point?" Chantel blurted.

"You can't have a child with a vampire male, no," Ceri shook her head, "but possibly with one of the shifters." She raised her brows.

Chantel pushed out a breath. "I don't think that is something that would interest me."

"You say that now, but things might change. You change as you get older, trust me. Not being able to have children never used to bug me much. It does now. Very much so. Give it a couple of years and you might change your mind."

"The kings keep talking of a program to bring our females and the shifter males together and yet it hasn't happened. It might never happen. There is too much animosity between the alphas and the kings."

"Far too much testosterone." Ceri smiled. "It could happen at some point though. Maybe not today and maybe not tomorrow, but sometime in the future. Point being, you could have young one day. It is in your grasp." Unlike her. Pain blossomed in her chest but she pushed it away, concentrating on the conversation.

Chantel nodded. "You're right."

"Be careful, that's all."

Chantel nodded again. She picked up the box of pills and then looked back at Ceri. "I will. I'll make them wear condoms as well."

"Good." Ceri smiled at the young female. "You do that."

"Thank you, healer. I appreciate it."

"You are most welcome," Ceri said, standing as the female did the same. "I will see you in a couple of months, unless you need help with anything."

Chantel turned to leave.

There was a knock at the door.

"Come in."

Drago stuck his head around the jamb, a grin plastered to his face. He sobered when he saw Chantel. "Sorry, I didn't know you were still busy." He turned his wrist, looking at his watch. "I thought you would be done by now."

"I am, Chantel was just leaving." Ceri glanced at the female who was blushing profusely. A reaction to Drago, for sure. The male was too good-looking for his own good. Females fell over their feet whenever he was near.

Thank fang she was immune, on account of them growing up together. He was more of a brother to her. Seeing him as anything other than that would be just plain nasty. It was funny watching Chantel though. The female knocked into Ceri's desk as she headed to the door, then giggled, finally waving as she left. Her cheeks a bright red.

"What's up?" Ceri asked, stacking some files. Trying to neaten her disaster of a desk.

"Thought you might want to," he shrugged, "head to Aorta this evening."

Ceri slumped her shoulders, feeling tired at the mere

thought of going to the nightclub.

"Really? You're going to drop me again. You never want to do anything anymore. It's all work, work, work."

"And with you, it's all play, play, play." She laughed at the look on Drago's face.

"Bullshit! I work plenty hard enough."

She nodded, having to concede. Not only was Drago handsome, he had brains and plenty of brawn too. Not nearly as much as the dragon—Why did she keep thinking about the shifter? Sure, they'd had a fun night together, but it was done and dusted. It should never have happened in the first place. Chantel had been right, the rifts between the species were still solidly in place. They didn't even know much about the dragon shifters, save that they were strong beyond measure. That they lived somewhere remote and unknown. That they didn't mix with other species as a rule. That was it. She had been right to leave the way she did, instead of finding out more about him. Ceri had wanted to know more. There had been questions buzzing around in her head. She'd even told him about not being able to have children. Ceri didn't normally talk about that. She'd been tempted to tell him her real name as well.

"Hello!" Drago waved a hand in front of her face. "Are you still in there?"

Oh shit! She had totally zoned out. "Yes." She nodded. "I'm just a little tired." Ceri yawned. Just talking about being tired made her feel tired.

"You need to get out and you need a good rut," Drago stated, quite matter-of-factly.

She shook her head. "Don't start on me." He'd been at her the whole of last week.

"I mean it." Drago narrowed his eyes into hers. "You

need sex and blood and lots of them both."

She hadn't felt much like drinking from anyone. Blood was bland and tasteless after…him…the dragon…Bay. Not that she had been able to actually consume much of his blood. It had been too much. An overload to her system. Addictive it would seem. Since blood didn't hold appeal now, neither did sex. *What was the point?* "I'm fine," she announced.

"You are not fine." He narrowed his eyes. "I mean, look at you." He waved a hand in her general direction. "You've lost weight. You hardly drink, you haven't rutted since you got back from vacation. You have dark circles under your eyes. You look like shit."

"Gee, thanks."

Drago chuckled. "Don't get me wrong, you're still gorgeous. You could have your pick of the males tonight. Come with me, dammit. Have some fun! Let your hair down. You'll get a whole lot further in breaking this depression you're in."

"I'm not depressed!" *How absurd!* Ceri just felt tired. She wanted blood alright but not from anyone in the coven. She wanted dragon blood. She needed to stop this! Going out with Drago would be the perfect way to do just that. *What was one night?* She was on the verge of agreeing to go when she realized she was being silly. She'd hate it at Aorta. Ceri didn't want to go. She shook her head. "No, thanks! Maybe next time." She was sure that given time, she would get over herself.

"You said that last time."

"I mean it this time."

"Why don't I believe you?" He pushed his hands into his pockets.

"No idea."

"Because you keep saying *'next time.'* You say it all the time lately. What the heck happened to you?" He took a seat, placing his foot on her desk.

"Careful!" She moved the stack of files away from his huge boot. He'd asked her this half a dozen times in the last month. Ceri sighed. "I told you—"

"If you say *'nothing'* I'll...I'll—"

"You'll what?" She rolled her eyes.

"I won't believe you, that's what." He sounded exasperated. "What happened? Ever since you got back from vacation you've been...different."

It was true. She *was* different. It felt like she'd become addicted to another species' blood. A species that wasn't reachable. A species her kings would not allow her to associate with. *Forget that!* Brant would have a shit fit if he ever found out she'd rutted a dragon, and that was putting it mildly. "Nothing happened." She tried to be forceful but failed.

"I know something happened and I wish you'd just tell me already so that we can fix it."

There was no fixing it. There was working through it, and that was on her, and on her alone. She didn't want to get Drago into any kind of trouble. "I'm fine." She reached over and gripped the side of his bicep. "I promise. There is just so much to do around here. Being a healer is not considered fashionable."

"Yeah, yeah, it's just you and a few of the elders. Not many of you, I know. You should look at trying to recruit more females."

She pushed out a breath. "Why does a healer have to be a female?"

He made a face. "You know I didn't mean it like that."

"I don't know what you meant. You do realize that

males would make good healers as well?"

"Absolutely." He nodded vigorously.

Ceri narrowed her eyes at him and whacked him on the side of his arm. "I mean it. That kind of thinking is sexist."

Drago dragged his boot off of the desk and used his arms to pretend to ward her off. "Don't hurt me." He grinned all the while.

Yeah, right! Like she could hurt him. An Elite. One of The Ten. He was full of shit. She laughed. He soon joined in. Drago sobered. "Look, if you say you're fine, then I have to respect that. You need to know that I'm here if you need anything though, okay?"

"Thanks. I appreciate it."

Drago stood up and enveloped her in a hug. "I mean it."

"I know."

He squeezed her tighter before letting her go.

CHAPTER 6

"Take a seat," Torrent grumbled, not looking up from his computer.

Bay did as he was commanded, watching as his king continued to type using only two fingers. It was painstakingly slow. Bay had to stop himself from fidgeting. From offering to help. He didn't dare though. He had a bad feeling about this meeting. By the way that Torrent was frowning, he was sure his gut was right on the money as well.

Bay had to work not to flinch when the Water king finally slammed his laptop shut. The male turned narrowed eyes on him. "What is going on with you?" he growled. Thankfully, Torrent didn't give him a chance to answer. In truth, Bay wasn't sure what he would say if he had. "You are screwing up at every turn." He pushed out a breath. "I know you are new at this role. I don't think you were…prepared for it. I'll admit that I threw you straight into deep water. You can't be blamed for that, but these are careless errors." He ran a hand through his hair, squeezing the back of his neck. "You sent one of the scouting teams into a '*no go*' zone. They were almost spotted by hunters."

"I know. I screwed up the coordinates. Sent them west

instead of east." Bay looked down at his lap for a second or two. "I don't want to make excuses, but—"

"Then don't!" Torrent all but yelled. "You took a male to task for not arriving for his shift when it was his day off. The list goes on. Stupid mistakes that make you look like a fool, not capable, and in turn it makes me look like a fool for appointing you to this role."

"My apologies, sire. I will be more diligent going forward."

"You had better, or I will be forced to make changes I'm not ready to make." Torrent shook his head. "I do not want to reinstate Flood. Maybe at some point in the future but not right now." It was made clear to him from the start that this was a temporary role. "Beck was just as much at fault. He disobeyed direct orders and that cannot be tolerated. I need you to step up and take charge for me. We are in dangerous and troubled times, I can't talk about it right now but…there are plans in motion. I require a strong leader. One who I can trust."

"I am the right male for the job." Under normal circumstances that would have been true. Right then, not so much. He needed to pull himself together!

"I hope so. Tide is…unavailable at present, particularly if there are trips involved."

"What kind of trips?" Bay frowned.

"I'm not ready to discuss it yet," Torrent growled. "Get your act together."

"Yes, sire." Again, Bay bowed his head for a moment. "You can count on me."

Torrent nodded once, opened his computer and went back to typing. Bay took that as a sign that he had been dismissed. "Thank you, sire." In truth, he was sure he had been about to be demoted. He was lucky…this time. Bay stood up and left, closing the door behind him.

Tide was standing just outside. The male winced as they locked eyes. "I couldn't help but overhear. Are you okay? Is there something I can help you with?"

"No, I'm fine. I'm still trying to get the hang of things, that's all."

Tide held his gaze for a while. "You seemed to be doing just fine. You were new to the role but managing, and then you went on the Stag Run. Things seemed to fall apart after that. Did something happen?"

"No!" Bay blurted a little too quickly. "Nothing happened." He folded his arms. "I mean, what could possibly have happened? Nothing that's what." He forced himself to shut the hell up.

Tide shook his head. "I don't know what could have happened. All I know is, you're acting like something did. Was it a female? I want to help you."

Bay shook his head. He didn't want anyone else to know what had gone down. Beck knew he had rutted someone, but that was it. No-one knew how much he was obsessing over this female. How he couldn't sleep. How if he did he would wake up in cold sweats. On the verge of coming and – at the same time – waking to the realization that finding completion would not be possible. It was frustrating as hell. How had it been possible?

How?

Could it happen again?

He also thought about her, not just the sex. Her eyes. Her smile. What was her name? It was the one thing about her that drove him to complete distraction. He had to know her name. So simple and yet—

"Look," Tide said, bringing him back from his reverie. The male looked up and down the hall. Bay did the same, noting they were alone. "It looks like you'll be going on a mission soon. Torrent is trying to pull me in on it, but I can't go. I have a private matter I need to attend to. He's expressed concern over taking you. He can't take Beck because it would mean undermining you, his defense leader."

Bay frowned. "If he did that the males would lose respect for me."

"Exactly! He'd have to demote you."

"Does that mean Flood's coming back?"

Tide shook his head. "No, he'll appoint someone new. Possibly put Beck in your position." The male shook his head. "He doesn't want to. It'll make him look bad. Like appointing you was a poor decision." Tide echoed what Torrent had said, which made him believe they'd discussed it. Of course they had. Tide was Torrent's second in command.

"I can do this," Bay said, more to himself than to Tide.

"I know you can." The male raised his brows. "It's not the easiest task, keeping two hundred headstrong males in line. Making them, not only do as you say, when you say it, but getting the most out of them at the same time. Getting them to go the extra mile for you...for our kingdom. I know you can do it though and you were managing adequately before. You were making good headway. That all stopped. I'd even say you've gone backwards. Pull it together." Tide gripped the side of his arm and squeezed. "I'm here if you need to talk...any time."

Bay nodded. "I appreciate it."

"This mission is a big deal. I'm sure Blaze will be involved."

Bay nodded. "I've got this!" He needed to sort his mind

out. To stay focused. Sleep would be good, but he'd cope. Maybe it was time to go to a healer for help. They could mix him an herbal tea or something. "I do!" he added, trying to convince himself.

CHAPTER 7

Ten days later…

Ceri looked across the table at the little boy. "Not hungry?" she asked, brows raised.

Sam shook his head. "I don't like broccoli," he announced, looking completely put out. Like his five-year-old world had just come to an end.

"You don't?"

He shook his head. "It tastes like poo."

Ceri had to laugh. How could she not? "What do you like to eat then?"

"Human blood." His eyes lit up.

She laughed even harder. "You do, do you?"

He nodded. "We sometimes get visiting humans. I bite them every chance I get."

Ceri felt her mouth drop open. "You don't!"

Sam nodded profusely. "Yes, I do."

"I'm sure your dads don't allow it." She looked at him skeptically, leaning her knife and fork on the sides of the plate.

Sam made a face. "No," he huffed. "I'm not allowed. I get into big trouble…" Then his eyes brightened. "But I do it anyway."

"You little rascal." She leaned forward and gave his cheek a light pinch.

Sam giggled. "Why do you do that? Every time I see you, you pinch my cheeks, Ceri."

"You have the cutest cheeks." She pinched them again. "So chubby and cute, just like the rest of you."

"Mummy is chubby." Sam shoved a big piece of chicken into his mouth and began to chew.

"She's not chubby, she's pregnant and there's a huge difference. Soon, you're going to have a brother. How exciting is that?"

He shrugged. "He won't be able to play with me."

"Not just yet, but soon enough."

Sam nodded. "I guess." He shoved another forkful of chicken into his mouth. "He's going to cry and poop a lot," he said, around his food.

Ceri laughed. "Definitely, but—"

There was a knock at her door. Two sharp raps and then the door opened before she could say anything. She knew exactly who was there. "Hi Brant," Ceri said, as he walked in.

Brant smiled. As always, her cousin was dressed to the nines. A three-piece suit, which fit him like a glove. A crisp, white shirt. A perfectly knotted tie. His shoes were shiny. His hair looked like it had been cut and styled that morning. "Ceri." He nodded in greeting, his expression morphed into one of utter joy as soon as he laid eyes on his son. "Hi, buddy."

"Daddy!" Sam yelled, his mouth still full. The little boy jumped off his chair and raced over to Brant, launching himself into his father's arms.

"Did you enjoy your playdate at your Ceri's house?"

Sam nodded. "We played cars and trains," he

announced.

"That sounds like fun!" Brant was smiling. The only other time Ceri saw the male this happy and carefree was when he was with his mate. Unless of course he and Zane were fighting, which happened from time to time. Being in a three-way mating sounded complicated if you asked her. Especially when the two males were both dominant. Both kings and used to being in charge. Certainly not for the faint of heart.

"It was fun!" Sam yelled.

"Are you ready to head home, bud?" Brant asked, putting Sammy down.

"Let him finish his lunch first. He still has a ton of broccoli to eat." She winked at Sam, whose face fell. The little guy started shaking his head, about to protest. "I'm only teasing," she quickly added with a laugh. "You don't have to eat the broccoli."

"You're evil." Brant cracked a smile. "Giving a child broccoli." He widened his eyes.

"I made the kind of lunch I would normally make for myself. I didn't give it much thought."

"Clearly." Brant raised his brows. "And talking about lunches, you need something a little more substantial than chicken, a spoonful of rice and broccoli. I can scent you haven't drank from anyone in a couple of days. You could definitely do with some liquid sustenance as well, or there is no point even eating solids."

"Chicken is healthy," she countered. "I'm seeing Drago later today," she continued. *Shit!* Now Brant was commenting on her weight loss as well. Had it got so bad that those around her were starting to pick up on it?

"You look like you could use some meat on your bones." He gave her the once over and she had her answer. "You're working too hard. Have no more trainees come forward?"

The chair scraped as Sam sat back down to his lunch.

She shook her head and locked eyes with her cousin and king of the vampires. "No-one wants to be a healer anymore. There are far more fascinating lines of work now that females are able to apply for any position they want. I'm still hoping to find a male willing to take on the role."

"You're still on about that?" Brant asked, one side of his mouth quirked up.

"I want to see males in traditionally female roles. There's nothing wrong with that."

"There is still a stigma attached. Males are afraid of being seen as pussies." He gave a one-shouldered shrug.

"Shhhhh." She put a finger in front of her mouth. "Language." She looked in Sam's direction.

"Please," Brant scoffed. "Have you heard how much Zane swears? Sammy knows he's not allowed to say those words until he's much older."

Ceri rolled her eyes. "You are a ruthless leader and yet your son has you wrapped around his finger."

"Shhh!!!" Brant's eyes widened. "Don't let him hear you say that."

"What?" She was smiling broadly. "Just in case he doesn't already know? I assure you he knows, no doubt about it."

Brant sighed. "You're right."

"How is Tanya doing? Did she have a good rest?"

Brant nodded. "Thank you for taking Sam for the afternoon, especially since this is your only day off. My mate really needed the break."

"Are you sure she's only eleven months along in this pregnancy? Between you and me, she looks like she should have had this baby already. I'm not sure how she's going to last one more month."

Brant widened his eyes. "Yeah, don't let her hear you say that. We had only just started trying for another child and she became pregnant. I have potent seed. So," he shook his head, "she's not further along."

"That's going to be one big boy then."

"He'll take after his father." Brant puffed out his chest.

"Or Zane – he could be the biological father this time around," she blurted, immediately kicking herself for opening her trap.

Brant's features tightened and his eyes darkened. "It doesn't matter who the biological father is."

"Of course not!" *Shit!* She'd ventured into touchy territory. There was no way to tell who the father was – biological father – they were both undoubtedly doting fathers to Sam. Even though Brant was the biological father, seeing as he was the spitting image of the male. Only once this child was born would they know for sure and even then, it might be impossible to tell just by looking at the baby.

"We're hosting a meeting between the species next week," Brant added out of nowhere.

"Oh." She tried to sound nonchalant, but her heart sped up just a touch. Why was he telling her this?

"Zane and I will be kept very busy during the three-day talks. I know you're busy too, but I'd appreciate it if you could keep an eye on Tanya. She won't ask for help, even if she desperately needs it."

"Sure, no problem. I would be happy to help out. I love Sammy."

"It's just that – as you know – we're very picky about

who looks after him. He is heir to the throne."

"Don't worry about it. I understand. I'll keep my eye on Tanya and help out with Sam."

Brant pushed out a breath. "Thank you." He nodded once.

"So, are all the species going to be there?" She had to know.

"Yes." Brant nodded. He stood up and looked over at Sam who was playing with his toy car rather than finishing his lunch.

"Even the elves?" She couldn't jump straight to the dragons or it might look suspicious.

"Yes, Keto will be attending. A couple of the alphas as well. We're allowing four delegates per species."

She smiled and nodded. "I'm sure the dragons won't be there." She laughed like it was a ludicrous idea.

"Actually, they are the ones who called for the meeting in the first place."

"Oh! Why is that?"

"It seems they are being harassed by dragon hunters. The dragons believe the rest of the species will also be targeted. That it's only a matter of time. Since we are still being harassed by factions that wish us harm, Zane and I thought it pertinent. Also, if we can help the dragons, maybe they will come to our aid in the future. You never know what might happen. We plan on keeping our enemies close."

"The dragons aren't our enemies though," she retorted.

"They're certainly not our friends." Brant's jaw tightened. "Let's see where they stand. We'll know soon enough."

"Surely you plan on using this to become allies...possibly even getting onto friendly terms with them?"

Brant choked out a laugh. "I highly doubt it, but you never know."

At least they were open to the possibility. Dragons were coming. Here. Four of them. There was just no way one of them could be Bay. *No way!* Her mouth watered just thinking about the male. Maybe she would crave dragon blood no matter who the male was. It was a sobering thought. She needed to stay far away. One thing was for sure, she didn't trust herself. Just thinking about dragon blood made her fangs descend. It wasn't getting any better. If anything, her need for their blood was getting worse. Her hunger growing by the day.

CHAPTER 8

Five days later…

F^{*uck!*} Why the hell was he being summoned? Things had been going better. His sleep had improved some since getting an herb draught from the healers. His mind still wandered to the vampire often, but he'd been able to clear his head, to remain more focused, at least during work hours. Alone, at home, was another story entirely but when it had counted, he had been attentive. There had been no more major screw-ups. At least, none that he knew of.

Bay continued to walk towards Torrent's office. His mind raced, going through each scenario. What could it be?

He sucked in a deep breath as he arrived at the large double doors that lead to his king's chamber. He knocked, waiting until he was called upon to enter.

Bay walked in, stopping in his tracks when he saw who was in attendance. "Good morning," he choked out when he finally found his faculties.

"Morning." Torrent nodded once.

"I'm not sure if you have met Blaze yet." Torrent

motioned to the male in question. King of all four dragon species.

Bay inclined his head. "I have never officially met you, my sire, no." He shook his head. "It is good to do so now, an honor."

Blaze held out his hand and Bay clasped it at the wrist. "Let's make it official then since we will be traveling together."

Bay's eyes widened and he nodded once. He had no idea what Blaze was talking about, only that it must be that mission Torrent had referred to the other day. "I am glad I can be of service," he stated simply, meaning it.

"This is Inferno, my younger brother, Prince of Fire. He will be accompanying us."

"You are going in Tide's place." Torrent didn't look happy about that fact. "We leave on Monday. The Water dragons were lucky enough to have been selected to accompany Blaze and Inferno on this mission."

"I am most honored," he addressed Torrent, turning to Blaze as he finished the sentence.

"We leave on Monday, giving us the weekend to prepare," Blaze stated.

"You will need to pack for three days," Torrent all but growled, still frowning heavily. "We are meeting with representatives of the other species to discuss the slayers. We feel that all the species are in danger."

His heart beat faster and his mouth suddenly felt dry. "All of the species?"

"That's what I said." Torrent narrowed his eyes.

"Yes, sire." Bay inclined his head. "Where are we meeting?" It was like he already knew the answer. Knew without a doubt where they were headed before anyone could say anything. His heart pounded in his chest anyway.

"To Sweetwater," Blaze said. "We are meeting on vampire territory. It is the most central. They have the most suitable accommodations as well."

Sweetwater.

Shit!

He was going to vampire territory. To her. To the female with the green eyes. Holy fucking shit!

"Bay!" Torrent snapped. "Are you listening?"

He swallowed thickly. "Yes, apologies!"

"Is there a problem?" Torrent asked. "Do you have something against vampires? If so, I can take Beck in your place."

"No!" he practically yelled. "No problem. I will be packed and ready. I look forward to attending the meeting. I'm sure the other species will be a big help in eradicating the hunters."

"A help," Blaze scoffed. "More like a hindrance. We don't need help from any of the others. We thought they needed to be informed. If they wish to aid us, then that is their decision and their right, but we don't need them. We are perfectly capable of dealing with this ourselves."

"Of course, my lord." He was screwing this up at every turn. He needed to keep his mouth shut and his ears open. Needed to stay focused!

"You have all the details," Blaze spoke to Torrent, who nodded. "We'll see you Monday first light?"

Torrent nodded again. "Good." Blaze gestured for Inferno to follow him. "Then we'll head out."

Once they were gone, Torrent turned to him. "Don't make me regret taking you on this mission. It is an honor that we were selected to accompany the Fire dragons. The other two tribes were not impressed, I can say that much." The male finally hinted at a smile. It didn't last. "Don't fuck this up. Stay close, keep your mouth shut and do as you are told."

Bay nodded. "Yes, sire. Understood." He bristled with excitement. He shouldn't, but he did. He had already made up his mind, he was going to find the female and find out everything he needed to know. On his off time, of course. There was no way this would interfere with the mission. He'd make sure of that. No-one even needed to know about any of it.

CHAPTER 9

Three days later…

No way. There was no way he was there. Ceri stood in one of the break rooms on the east side of the castle. It gave her the perfect view of the conference center. Her kings had built the facilities when they had started The Program. A plan geared up to pair the top vampire males with human females, in the hopes they would mate and have young. So far, The Program had been a great success.

She forced herself to concentrate because the delegates attending the meeting between the species were going to file out at any minute.

She shouldn't be there. This was stupid and silly and made no sense. Out of all the dragon shifters out there, only four were on vampire soil at the moment. There was just no way he was one of the four, and if he was, she couldn't do anything about it. She needed to stay far away. It didn't matter, because he wasn't there, which would make staying away easy. She just needed to see that with her own eyes, so that she could stop wondering.

Ceri glanced at her watch, the second hand counted

down to one o'clock. As the hand hit twelve, the door opened. Ceri shook her head. Brant was running the event, so it stood to reason that the whole thing would run this smoothly.

Brant's PA came out, standing next to the open door, she held a clipboard in her hand. Three males filed out shortly after. They wore jeans and button-down shirts. They were followed by Zane who wore his standard leathers. Then two really large males appeared. They were wearing cotton pants. Their chests were golden. Her heart beat faster.

Dragon shifters. If the accounts had been correct, this was the standard attire of a dragon shifter. A tall dark-haired male followed closely behind. That made three. One more to—

No!

Come on!

She squealed and clasped a hand over her mouth. It was him. It was Bay. Of all the males, it was him. What a bizarre twist of fate. She noticed how he looked around, his eyes flashing to the castle, where they stayed for a few moments. It almost felt like he was looking directly at her. Her eyes felt wide. Her skin prickled. Then he looked away and moved off. Several other males had walked out, they followed behind Bay. Heading towards the restaurant where they would serve lunch.

Everything in her told her to go. To find a way to grab his attention. Maybe get a server to hand him a note.

No!

She'd made up her mind. There would be no fraternizing with the dragon shifters. Most especially, no fraternizing with him. She turned away from the window, even though she could still see his retreating form. She clenched her hands into fists and forced herself to walk the other way.

CHAPTER 10

They were being housed in a hotel, separate from the vampire castle. There were a few vampires around. They worked as staff in the hotel and conference area. Servers, receptionists and housekeepers. Bay kept hoping he would see her. So far, no luck. Chances were good he wasn't going to have much luck either.

He was tempted to ask, maybe someone knew her, but he didn't want to draw attention to himself and definitely not to her. He had no idea what her name was or what she did. Who she was.

No idea.

No clue.

It was frustrating. The castle was big, with more than one entrance. It had four huge towers and an enormous central section. According to the vampire server he had questioned, it even had several floors underground. He shuddered at the thought. Dragons weren't partial to confined spaces. Point being, his mystery female could be anywhere. In any one of the many rooms.

Bay forced his attention back to what was happening around him. He took a final bite of his steak and pushed the half-eaten meal aside. His stomach churned.

So far, the species meeting had gone well. After the initial introductions, Blaze had explained the history between the dragons and the hunters, as well as all the background information about the hunters. All fairly boring.

Inferno bumped the side of his arm. "Aren't you going to eat that?" He pointed his fork at Bay's plate.

Bay shook his head. "No, it's beef." He made a face, "I much prefer deer steak. Not as tender but far tastier." It was true, he did prefer deer meat, but that wasn't the reason he didn't want the food.

"Mind if I…?" The male raised his brows. He looked down at Bay's steak, his fork already in the meat.

Bay nodded once. "Take it," he mumbled.

Inferno grinned, taking the meat and dumping it on his own plate. He sliced a large piece. "I can't believe both of those males rule." He gestured to where Brant and Zane were standing. The vampire kings.

Bay shrugged. "We have four kings."

"Yes, but Blaze is the ultimate decision maker. The vampires rule equally. Not only that," his voice dropped a few octaves, "they share a female."

Bay raised his brows. "Now that is strange." He couldn't imagine. He scrutinized the males. They were very different. Brant was tall and although built, he didn't come across as a warrior. He wore fancy human clothing. Gold glinted on his cuffs. The male was what females would consider to be good-looking.

Zane was the opposite. Not as tall but extremely honed. The male looked ready for battle in his leather clothing. There was a curved sword slung across his back. His hair was cut close to his scalp. Nothing fancy about him. Hard and rugged. So different and yet they had made it work.

Sharing a female. Bay couldn't imagine it. Dragons didn't share. *Forget it!*

Two more vampires sat at the end of the table. They had been introduced as York and Gideon. They were the leaders of the vampire warriors. He hadn't figured out yet who outranked whom. They wore the same clothing as Zane.

The elves sat to one side, dressed in silk attire. Their heritage evident by their pointy ears and long hair. The king wore a simple, gold crown. They ate large bowls of sliced fruit and kept to themselves. So far, they hadn't interacted much, and they spoke in hushed tones.

To Inferno's left were the shifters. All alphas. They wore human attire. Jeans and button-down shirts. Only two of the males talked together. The other two kept their distance. One even sat away from the rest. It was clear that there was no love lost between them. Right then, he was thankful that the dragon kingdoms had put aside their differences. It was vital if they were to stand against the hunters.

"So next, Blaze is going to talk everyone through the interactions with the hunters to date."

Bay nodded. There had been a number of incidents over the last year. "Yeah, then there'll be a Q & A session before breaking for the day."

"Tomorrow, we discuss the way forward and how we can work together to stop the slayers."

The shifter next to them snorted. Bay couldn't remember his name. Inferno tensed, his eyes narrowing for a moment before slicing off another piece of meat and eating it.

"I'm not too sure about team-building activities." Bay raised his brows. "What kind of activities? Who decided on the program?"

"The bloodsuckers," the shifter grumbled. "It's stupid! I will be leaving long before then."

"We're here to unite against a common enemy," Bay said.

"Bullshit." The shifter sat back in his chair. "These hunters are *your* enemy. Not mine!"

"They potentially—" Inferno started.

"You call them slayers. Dragonslayers...*dragon* being the operative word. You dragons are trying to get the other species to do *your* bidding."

Inferno's whole frame tightened. He shoved his plate to the side even though he hadn't finished what was left of the meal.

Bay didn't like where this was going. "We thought it pertinent that the rest of the species were aware of the hunters," he interjected.

"Well, isn't that nice of you."

Inferno nodded. "Yes, actually I do think—"

"Bull! You want us to fight your battles for you. It's clear from the few interactions we have had with your species that you think yourselves far superior to the rest of us. I thought the bloodsuckers were bad, I—"

"Stop calling the vampires that!" Bay spoke softly. "I'm not sure why you're so angry but—"

"Don't tell me what to do, dragon. You don't call the shots, even if you think you do. Let me ask you something, where were the dragons when we were being stalked by the Feral? When our people were being abducted? Where were you then?" Bay had heard of the Feral. They were griffin shifters. They were an elusive species who kept strictly to themselves. They were strong, fast and deadly.

"We only heard about the abductions after—" Inferno

began.

"I don't want to hear excuses," the male snapped, pushing his chair back. "When we needed help, there was no-one to be seen. Now that you are the ones in trouble, we're all expected to drop everything. It's typical!" he spat, looking royally pissed off. "I had to leave my mate and my cub for this." He snorted.

"If you feel so strongly about it, why are you even here?" Inferno growled. The male was bristling.

Bay needed to stop this before one of them lost their temper. "Maybe we should all calm down."

"Don't tell me what to do!" The shifter's face was red, his shoulders were tense. His hands curled into fists.

Inferno's jaw was tight, his eyes were bright with anger as well.

The shifter locked eyes with Inferno. "Why I am here is none of your damned business." The shifter spoke under his breath. Why was he so angry? "All you need to know is that I wish I wasn't. I knew it would be a waste of time, and it is. You scaly assholes can fight your own damned—"

"What the fuck did you call me?" Inferno yelled as he pushed his own chair back, jumping to his feet.

The shifter did the same.

Inferno was a hothead. "Wait!" Bay tried.

"You heard me." The shifter was also on his feet, bumping chests with Inferno.

The other males in the room stopped what they were doing and silence befell the room.

"Don't," Inferno snarled.

"I called you a scaly assh—" the shifter didn't get to finish. A white-hot blast left Inferno's mouth. The flames engulfed the area. Bay fell backwards to avoid being burned, landing flat on his back.

The ceiling was scorched. No longer a pristine white, it had streaks of black. One section smoldered. Smoke filled the room. He coughed as he moved to his feet. Then it started. The screaming. Loud shrieks of agony.

The shifter was rolling around on the ground. His hands clutched to his face. His shirt was burned off around the neck and chest. His skin red and blistered. His long hair burned. His scalp, red and flaking.

His face.

More screaming.

"What the fuck?" one of the shifters snarled as he rushed over to the downed shifter.

"I told you bringing Cooper was a bad idea," the bear shifter announced, stuffing his hands into his pockets. "I heard the last part of the exchange and he had it coming."

"Yes, but," Blaze looked pissed, "was that level of retaliation completely necessary?" He spoke to Inferno.

"Yes, that fucker needed to be brought down a rung or two," Inferno snarled. "For a moment he forgot who he was talking to."

"That was one of the highest-ranking alphas," one of the shifters announced. "Many seasons your senior."

"Leave it, Ward." The bear shifter put a hand on Ward's chest.

Inferno snorted. "I am Prince of Fire. I outrank an alpha by a long shot." He said *alpha* like it was an insult.

The shifter on the ground continued to writhe and scream, his hands still plastered over what was left of his face. It looked melted. His eyes were gone, a hole in the place of his nose.

"We need to help...him." Bay pointed at the shifter. Trying to redirect the male's attention. This whole situation could become ugly and fast. Inferno still looked angry. So did the wolf alpha, Ward.

"Yes, you are right," Brant said, moving forward. "He needs to see the healers. They can mix him something for the pain and dress those wounds. Make it bearable for him during the healing process."

Bearable.

Bay doubted anything a healer could do would make that bearable. Torrent looked on, a look of distaste on his face.

"He should be left to suffer," Inferno barked. "He deserves it."

"Stop!" Blaze commanded, his eyes on Inferno.

Inferno narrowed his eyes as well. "I am well—"

"I said to stop." More evenly delivered this time. Somehow more forceful.

"You take his feet," Ward instructed the bear shifter.

"I'll take him." Bay stepped forward. He picked up the still screaming male, trying not to cause further damage.

"Follow me." Brant looked indifferent. Completely calm. "I'll show you the way."

Bay nodded, having to hold on tight as the male continued to twist and turn in his hold.

"I have scheduled for you to undergo the procedure tomorrow at ten. You should be here an hour before, to get settled in."

This was the worst part about her job, hands down. It was part of the reason why she struggled to find young healers. Most of the healers were elderly and getting ready to retire. It was a dire situation.

Angelique's lip quivered. "Are you sure there is no

other way?"

Ceri shook her head. "The child is as good as lost already."

The female made a sobbing noise and covered her mouth, "I can't believe I was so careless."

"You had your partner wear a condom."

"Yes, but," tears ran down her cheeks, "it broke. I should have gone on the birth control like you said. I was stupid and now." She put a hand to her belly.

"I know, it's difficult. This will be one of the hardest things you will ever have to endure." She leaned forward and took Angelique's hand. "It's not your fault your pelvis is narrow. Not your fault you can't birth this baby. You have a good chance of dying if you try to have this child. The baby will most certainly die. The only recorded cases where the baby survived, was because the mother gave her life to make it so, and even then, it's not always successful."

The young female whimpered softly and nodded her head. "I have no choice then?"

Ceri pulled in a deep breath. "I'm afraid not."

Angelique bit down on her bottom lip and nodded again. Tears coursed down her cheeks.

"You will—"

The door to her office flew open and an unknown male, a shifter walked in. "What is the meaning of this. You can't just—"

"One of our visitors needs your help," Brant growled as he walked through the entrance as well.

Bay!

Her heart sped up. Had something happened to Bay? "What is…? Was the—?"

Thank god! She caught sight of him carrying a male. Her

heart felt like it was slamming against her ribcage as his intense blue eyes caught hers. He stopped in his tracks but quickly picked up the pace again.

"I'll see you tomorrow," Angelique said, already walking.

"Yes. Stay strong," Ceri called after her.

Then she caught his scent and despite the audience, her fangs erupted. Try as she might, she couldn't get them to retract. Hopefully, her king would assume it was the strange species and the severity of the situation. Sometimes an adrenaline spike could cause a physical reaction as well. "What the hell happened?" she snarled, as adrenaline flooded her system. "Who hurt him?"

"One of the Fire dragons. There was an argument." Brant said.

One of the shifters snorted, looking angry.

The male in Bay's arms was screaming, his hands clutched to his burned face. Despite the scent of wolf, bear and charred flesh, she could still get his scent. It seemed to rise above everything else.

Chili, dark chocolate and smoke.

Her mouth watered. *Focus, Ceri!* This was no time to lose it. Her nail beds tingled. Hopefully her eyes were normal. Her irises still green instead of blood red. Her breathing was elevated, as was her heart-rate but again, that could be blamed on the situation.

"Put him on the bed!" she instructed.

The male continued to writhe. "Do something!" the wolf shifter shouted at her as Bay put the male down.

"Do not use that tone with me, or I will ask you to leave," she snapped, already moving to the bed so that she could examine the shifter.

"Ceri," Brant warned.

She wasn't about to apologize. This was her office and she wasn't going to accept being ordered around by a wolf.

She could feel the dragon's eyes on her. Could hear the rush of his blood and the beat of his heart. Could feel the warmth radiating off his body even though he was a few feet away. Her fangs throbbed, making it hard to concentrate. Thankfully he moved away, just a little. Giving her the space she needed to be able to form coherent thoughts.

When she looked down, she saw that her nails had sharpened. *Shit!* She needed to control this. She was so thirsty…for dragon blood. For his blood. *Concentrate on the job at hand!*

Ceri began her assessment of the male, he was badly burned. To the extent that even if she knew who he was, she probably wouldn't be able to recognize him. He was in agony. Ceri switched on the kettle which was still lukewarm from the cup of tea she had made earlier. "I'm going to make a strong herbal tea. It'll take a couple of minutes. Then you'll have to hold him down so that I can get the mixture down his throat. It will knock him out cold for at least an hour, possibly even two. Then I'll be able to dress his wounds. It'll help speed up the healing process as well and soothe the wounds when he wakes up. At least the worst of the pain will have subsided by then. The healing process will be well on its way."

She assembled what she needed as she spoke, placing the leaves she needed into a beaker. Two shifter males held the shifter down.

"What is his name?" She gestured with her eyes to the injured male, having to speak up to be heard above the moans. Thankfully he had stopped screaming.

"Cooper," the wolf shifter said, not looking up. "It's

okay," he soothed the male. "The healer will help you."

"Can I assist in any way?" Bay asked, stepping towards her.

"No!" she all but yelled, trying not to breathe, and turning from the dragon. Ceri swallowed thickly. "Thank you," she added, not wanting to seem rude. "I'll manage," she mumbled. Thankfully he moved back. Ceri pulled in a deep breath through her mouth. Good lord, but she could taste him on her tongue. She almost groaned out loud. She felt her nails lengthen and sharpen.

"How is he?" a male asked from the doorway, dragging her attention back to the problem at hand. It was another dragon shifter. This one had a golden chest.

"How do you think he is?" the bear shifter snarled.

"Let's keep this cordial," Brant interjected.

"One of your males," the bear pointed at the male at the door, "did this, and over nothing!"

"It wasn't exactly over nothing." When Bay spoke, gooseflesh rose up on her arms. "Your male said some things he shouldn't have. I'd say that the response was a little harsh but—"

"A little harsh?" the bear snapped. "I'd say you're underestimating the situation."

"Stop!" Ceri interrupted. "I have a job to do and this isn't the time to argue." She finished straining the leaves. The water had turned a bright green color. She added a few ice cubes from the freezer. They clinked as she stirred the liquid. She added a few more, going through the motion. Repeating the process one more time until the herb mixture was cool enough to drink.

By then the downed shifter was moaning and mumbling incoherently. When she moved to the side of the bed, she realized just how badly he had been maimed.

His lips were gone, leaving his teeth exposed in what looked like a grimace. "I'm going to give him all of this." She held up the beaker. "I'll need to use a syringe." He wouldn't be able to drink it down without a mouth, without lips.

Ignore the dragon.

Ignore him!

Her fangs were still elongated. Still throbbing. If anyone noticed, they didn't say anything. Maybe it wasn't as bad as she thought. She took a syringe from her supply cupboard and headed back to the bed. Then she sucked up some of the liquid. "I'm trying to help you, Cooper."

The male continued to mumble and moan.

"You need to drink this. It will knock you unconscious for a while." She spoke clearly and concisely. She wasn't sure whether he had heard her or not. "You may need to hold him." She spoke to the males at the bed. Both were frowning deeply, looking greatly concerned over their downed friend. "Take his shoulders…carefully," she added when she saw the burns there as well. Not as bad as his face, but still. "You need to lift him a little so that he can drink without choking."

"I know how he feels," the dragon at the door said. "Poor bastard."

Once the males had him up slightly, Ceri put the syringe tip between the male's teeth and slowly depressed the plunger.

The male spluttered and choked but he also swallowed. "Another one," she urged, placing another full syringe between his teeth and slowly pushing. They went through the process several more times. "That's enough." She motioned for the shifters to lower Cooper.

"What's wrong with your eyes?" the bear shifter asked.

"Nothing," she mumbled.

"No really, they're a little on the red side and don't tell me they're bloodshot because I've seen bloodshot and that's not what it looks like." The shifter narrowed his eyes at her, distrust evident.

"It's a tense situation. High octane, high adrenaline," she said, looking away.

The bear's jaw tensed and then he nodded. "You seem calm enough."

"Like a duck," she countered. "He's unconscious." Ceri pointed at Cooper.

"I want that male punished." The bear pointed at the dragon who was still at the door.

"He will be."

"I mean it, Torrent!" the bear yelled. "And a public apology."

"They had a squabble. Some things were said. It happened in the heat of the moment."

"Bullshit!" the same shifter countered, pointing a finger at Torrent.

"Stop!" She wanted to roll her eyes. This was probably how the initial squabble had started in the first place. "That's enough." The last thing she wanted was to have to treat any more burn victims. One was bad enough. At least the male was oblivious to the pain now. She needed to prepare another herbal tea, ready for when he woke up. She'd make it a little weaker this time. She also needed to dress the wounds in an aloe and tea tree salve.

His scent hit her nostrils. Her nipples tightened and her fangs throbbed. "Out!" she shouted, panicking when she realized how close he was and how thirsty she had become. It was worse than ever. She could feel the last couple of weeks acutely. The longing, the hunger, the need. The lack of blood. *Thirsty.* She was so thirsty. Her mouth dry. Her throat raw and burning. Her stomach hollow.

"I was about to—" He was coming closer. She was afraid of what she might do if he came too close. Her nails were long. Her fangs throbbing. Her eyes were probably all out red. She turned to her herb shelf, away from the males in the room. Away from him.

"Out!" she yelled again. "Everyone. Get out now! He needs to rest."

"But—" the bear shifter began.

"You can come back in two hours to check on him. Now go!"

"Are you sure I can't help?" Bay asked. That voice coupled with his scent. Need coursed through her.

"I'm fine!" she snapped. "He's asleep. I don't need help."

"You said you had to dress his wounds," Bay added.

She glanced his way, noticing the look of concern on his face. "Thank you." She swallowed again, her throat felt not just dry but raw. "I can manage on my own. I would prefer it."

"Are you alright, Ceri?" Brant asked.

"Fine. I have a lot to do. That's all." She began to gather items she needed for the salve. "I need to cancel my next couple of appointments. Need to treat Cooper." She gestured towards the shifter, all the while praying they would leave already.

"Are you sure you don't need help?" Bay asked.

"Yes, I'm positive!" she tried not to sound angry and failed.

"Let's give the healer some space," Brant said. "Under the circumstances, I think we should cancel the rest of today's proceedings," his voice grew softer as he turned his back and headed for the door, "give everyone a chance to calm down. We'll pick back up where we left off tomorrow."

"Sounds like a good idea," the dragon, Torrent said.

She glanced over her shoulder. Bay had moved back but he was still looking her way. His eyes lit up and he stepped towards her, pulling in a breath. He was about to say something. The raging need inside her had become like a piercing scream. She'd do just about anything to stop it. She turned away, ignoring him. Praying with all her might that he would take a hint.

She had to hold back a loud sigh as she heard him retreat. Ceri concentrated, instead, on gathering the items she needed to make the salve. Her heart beat rapidly and her mind raced.

She was going to call Drago and organize to go out with him at the end of her shift. It was time to get over this problem of hers. What scared her more than anything was that she'd caught the scent of the male at the door, Torrent, and it had held no interest to her. The male was also a dragon shifter and yet, he held no interest at all. Panic welled. She needed to get over Bay as a matter of extreme urgency.

CHAPTER 11

"That was a fucking stupid thing to do," Blaze chided Inferno. "I agree with the bear shifter, you will need to apologize to that male."

"Not a fuck!" Inferno growled, folding his arms. "He can forget it. He called us scaly assholes and said that all we wanted was the for rest of the species to do our bidding."

Blaze scoffed. "That's exactly what we want," he announced. "And technically we do have scaly assholes, at least some of the time. It was no reason to burn his face off."

"The male was being derogatory. He deserved what he got. He'll think twice before mouthing off to one of us again." Inferno puffed out his chest.

"You will apologize and then we will proceed with the meeting," Blaze commanded. He narrowed his eyes on Inferno. "I have made up my mind," he added, there was a growly edge to his voice.

Inferno's jaw clenched but he didn't say anything. The male was probably thinking what Bay was thinking, that Blaze had lost his temper and had done the same thing on more than one occasion. The Fire king had never apologized to any of the males he had burned to a crisp.

Not even once. He'd never even hinted at an apology.

"I want you to go back to your hotel," Blaze continued, "and I want you to stay in your suite until we meet back tomorrow."

"What about dinner?" Inferno asked.

"Use room service," Blaze countered.

"I had planned on rutting one of the vampire females. That will be difficult if I can't go out and meet any." Inferno looked sulky.

"What?" Blaze snarled. "Head out of the gutter! You are not permitted to rut with anyone while here. Vampires are off limits. A hard no! This isn't a Stag Run. And while we're at it," Blaze turned to Bay; the king's eyes widened and he sucked in a breath. "Never mind," he mumbled as he realized who he was talking to. When he remembered Bay couldn't rut with anyone. That it wasn't possible.

Inferno looked completely affronted. He frowned and then looked as if he wanted to say something and then frowned again. Eventually, his shoulders slumped and he nodded once.

"You are dismissed," Blaze said. "Straight to your room," he added.

"I'm not six anymore. I'm not the young boy you used to pick on and tease. You might be my king, but—"

"Stop acting like a whelp and I'll stop treating you like one," Blaze growled back at his brother.

Inferno stalked off. His face was red and his jaw clenched.

"Why didn't you intervene?" Torrent asked him. "You might have been able to stop the whole thing."

For a second, Bay couldn't believe what he was hearing. "I tried, but—"

"Not hard enough." Torrent looked pissed.

Bay couldn't believe he was getting the blame for this as well. He'd had nothing to do with it.

"Can I trust you not to get yourself into any more trouble?" Torrent raised his brows.

"With all due respect, my lord, I didn't cause any trouble. I tried to intervene but they were going to fight no matter what I said or did. Both of them were looking for it. In answer to your question, yes, you can absolutely trust me because unlike, Inferno and Cooper, I'm not looking for trouble."

Torrent frowned. *Shit!* Maybe he shouldn't have said anything? No, he should have. Sure, he'd made some mistakes, but he wasn't a hothead troublemaker. He was well within his rights to stand up for himself.

Torrent finally narrowed his eyes a little and then nodded. "Don't let me down."

"I won't." Bay shook his head.

"Blaze and I have a couple of things to discuss. I plan on ordering in tonight as well, so I'll see you tomorrow."

Bay nodded.

With that, the two males turned and left. Bay felt both good and bad and all at the same time. Good because he had stood up to Torrent and – in his opinion – had won. Bad because he did plan on making trouble. Well, not exactly trouble. He planned on going to see Ceri.

Ceri.

He knew her name and it was beautiful. Suited her. Bay had almost fallen on his face when he had seen her. He all but forgot the shifter in his arms. A healer. *Wow!* That suited her too. It had been a struggle to contain himself. Not to give himself away, at any rate. She'd looked upset right from the start. Aside from one or two sideways glances, she'd ignored him flat.

There were a couple of things he needed to know. By now she would be finished or almost finished with Cooper. If not, he was going to help her, whether she liked it or not, and then they were going to talk. She'd canceled all her appointments and had sent the alphas away for two hours. They had plenty of time.

Once Bay made up his mind, he had to force himself to walk calmly. If it were up to him, he'd run and as fast as his legs could carry him. He'd found her, by some miracle, he'd actually found her. Bay walked quickly, making it back to her office in no time.

He knocked twice and entered before she could say anything.

Ceri dropped the bandages she had been carrying. Her eyes widened and she sucked in a breath. "What…?" she said, looking stricken. "What are you doing here?" Then she narrowed her eyes like she was angry with him. "You should leave," she went on to say, before he could answer.

"I just want to talk." He put up a hand, wanting to placate her.

Ceri was breathing quickly. It looked like she was breathing through her mouth. "Are you okay?" He walked into the office, closing the door behind him. Her dark hair was tied in a ponytail. She wore a white coat that did a good job of covering up her beautiful body. It didn't matter, he could easily remember exactly how she looked under all the layers. Bay swallowed thickly. His coming here wasn't about that. About sex. He swallowed again, feeling need coil inside him nonetheless. Of course, that's where it ended. No blood flowed south. For once he was happy about the fact.

"Why are you here?" She looked afraid. *Why was she afraid?* Surely not of him? He didn't like it. "You need to leave right now." She pointed at the door, taking a step back.

Bay shook his head. He frowned. "Why? I don't understand. I'm here to talk. Just to talk," he said as he walked towards her. It left him feeling…off-kilter that she was treating him this way. Like he had done something wrong. "I only need a few minutes of your time." He took another step towards her. "Please."

It happened quickly. Her eyes turned blood red. Her canines elongated into long, sharp fangs. Ceri snarled as she leaped, closing the five feet between them with one single jump. He was so shocked, that when her feet hit his chest, he fell backward. She was on him in an instant. Her fangs sinking into his neck. Her claws into his shoulders.

Ceri sucked hard. He felt the blood leave him on a hard pull…felt that pull all the way to the tip of his cock, right into his sac, which pulled painfully tight in an instant. Ceri moaned deeply as she sucked a second time. Long and hard. Bay grit his teeth, trying not to come. Thankfully she broke contact with a hard yell.

Bay rolled her onto her back. Her eyes were still mostly red, hints of green had bled their way back into her irises though. Dark tendrils had broken free from her ponytail. She was still breathing heavily. Her fangs looked deadly. His blood on her lips. Bay was fucked if the sight of her like that didn't turn him on more. He hadn't thought it possible, but it happened.

She reached up and palmed his cock. Any semblance of control left him then and there. He growled fiercely as he ripped her white coat. She yanked at his pants, grabbing his dick as soon as it was free. Her nails were long and sharp, but he was a sick bastard because it felt good. Bay groaned, feeling need coil in the pit of his stomach. His gums itched and his teeth sharpened some.

One hard upward pull and her dress was torn on one side and yanked up around her hips, giving him access to her pussy. No underwear this time. Her legs folded around his hips, her shoes dug into his ass. Ceri made desperate little noises that were driving him insane. Her nails were digging into his shoulders.

He thrust into her with a loud snarl. Her pussy was wet and tight.

Shit!

Shit!

Shit!

He struggled to hold it together, wanting so badly to come, then and there. With a rough grunt, he began to thrust. *Fuck!* He wasn't going to last long. *No chance!* Not when he was this desperate.

Thankfully, Ceri was moaning deeply. He found her clit and rubbed on it. Her moans intensified. Her pussy tightened some more around him, which made him growl. A deep vibration that ended in a snarl as he blew. Bay called her name. Her real name. He hadn't meant to, it just happened. Her pussy all out strangled him and she screamed, bowing her back. Then she bit down on him, sucking another gulp of his blood.

Bay roared. He felt such intense pleasure that it was on the verge of being painful. Every muscle pulled tight. Her pussy spasmed just as hard. Ceri groaned so loudly her throat had to hurt.

Bay thrust slowly a few more times and then stopped moving. They were both breathing heavily. Ceri swallowed thickly. Her eyes were hazy when she opened them. Then she blinked a couple of times and they widened. She got this shocked expression and pushed at his chest. "Get off me!" she yelled.

Bay pulled out and moved away. Looked like he had found trouble despite the fact that he hadn't been looking for it. Ceri seemed upset. That, and pissed.

Ceri scrambled up, pulling her dress down and yanking her coat closed. "Shit!" she cursed. "Why did you come back? I told you to leave." She felt panicked. Only because she was still aroused. And maybe because she wanted more. Lots more! More sex. More blood. More of him. "Now look what's happened. Dammit!" She paced away from him. Why had he come back? Why? This was going to make it more difficult to get over him. To move on. She barely knew him and—*Arghhh,* this was a mess.

"I'm sorry!" he said, adjusting his pants and getting to his feet. He was even more attractive than she'd remembered. Those gorgeous blue eyes seemed to look right into the heart of her. His hair was tousled, his silver chest gleamed. His shoulders impossibly broad. So damned sexy. So delicious! *What was she thinking?* She couldn't think like that about a dragon. Bay was still aroused as well, which wasn't helping things.

"Leave now!" Then she realized that if he left, everyone would know what had gone down between them. Brant would have a shit fit of epic proportions. She scrubbed a hand over her face. "No wait!" she said, not that he was going anywhere. "You can't leave just yet, we need to get the scent of…what just happened off of our skin. Then you need to go. I can't ever see you again!" She sounded downright nasty, but it couldn't be helped.

"Well, it's nice to see you too." His eyes clouded, making her feel terrible. *No!* It was for the best for both of them. This couldn't happen again. It should never have happened in the first place.

She pushed out a breath and shook her head. "I definitely can't say the same. This should never have happened." She shook her head.

"You're acting like this is my fault. You were the one who attacked me. Or was it all a figment of my imagination?"

She ignored the comment, only because she couldn't say anything back. It was all true. She had pretty much attacked him. Her face felt warm just thinking about it.

"I came here to talk, that's all," Bay went on, "I wanted to ask you something and maybe say hi. Then you jumped me."

"And you hated every minute. That's why you had me on my back in a second."

"You stuck your fangs into me first."

"Whatever," she mumbled as she walked to the door, locking it. Then she closed the blinds all the way. Praying no-one had seen anything. Praying even harder that they would get away with this. "This is such a mess. I haven't even finished dressing his wounds. What if someone comes here? One of those shifters? Your dragon buddies? My cousin."

She watched his eyes dart around the room. "Who is your cousin?" She could see his mind working.

"Brant."

Bay swallowed thickly. "I would be in serious trouble." He cleared his throat. "Make that, I'm going to be in serious trouble. They will be sure to smell it on us."

"Not necessarily."

"What do you mean?"

She walked over to where she kept her herbs and spices.

Instead of going to the shelving, she went to a plant growing in the corner. It was a succulent of sorts. Somewhere between a cactus and a regular plant. It had long thick leaves that grew three feet high. They were dark green with a waxy surface. She cut off one of the leaves and got to work, chopping and peeling. Using the pestle and mortar, she crushed the pieces into a gloopy pulp which she poured into a bowl. Crushing each piece until there was quite a substantial amount of the goo. Certainly enough for the two of them to get rid of each other's scent.

"We need to wash with this…all over and quick." She glanced at the door. "Before someone comes." Then she glanced over at Cooper. The male was still unconscious.

"This is going to work at removing the scent of our rutting?" He looked skeptical.

"Yes. I've never tried it myself, but it apparently works. Someone I know used it a couple of times. The shifters know about it."

"Shifters?" He frowned, shaking his head. "What do shifters have to do with anything?"

"Long story, but one of our males mated a wolf shifter. They used it to keep their relationship a secret. It works! At least," she raised her brows, "I think it does. It should." She shrugged.

"Okay, let's try it. It's not like we have anything to lose."

"You go first." She handed him the bowl.

Bay took it. "You said you're worried someone might come. Let's get this over with. I'll wash your back and you can wash mine." The one side of his mouth quirked up. Why was he trying so hard to be nice to her?

Ceri was still painfully aware of how attracted to him

she was. She shook her head. "No, I need to finish putting salve on Cooper's wounds."

Bay glanced over at the downed shifter. "It looks like you took care of the worst of them already." He probably knew she was making excuses.

His face was dressed in gauze and bandages that had been soaked in the salve. There was a thick layer beneath the bandages. She had applied the ointment to the wounds on his neck and chest, but she still wanted to dress them as well. At the same time, she was worried someone might come. That one of the shifters or, heaven forbid, her cousin might ignore her earlier request and come by anyway.

"We've rutted on two occasions now," the dragon said. "I've seen you naked. I've been inside you, for claw's sake. Let's do this thing."

Ceri nodded. "Fine! Let's make it quick. I can wash my own back," she snapped.

"Fine," he growled, following behind her.

Ceri started the shower, adjusting the temperature. She was lucky there was even a shower at her offices. She often worked late and washed there before heading out. Back in the days when she still actually went out, that is.

She pulled off the coat and peeled off the torn dress, placing the garments neatly on the closed toilet lid. She prayed she had a spare white coat in the cupboard in her office. One thing at a time. They needed to get clean.

When she glanced back at Bay, she noticed his mouth hung open, his eyes glued on her ass.

He seemed to snap out of it as soon as he caught her gaze, quickly pulling his cotton pants down his thighs. His thick member sprang free, jutting proudly from his body. His eyes were heated, his gaze stern.

Her nipples tightened and her mouth felt dry as a bone. It didn't help that she couldn't take as much as she would have liked from him. What was she saying? She shouldn't have taken any. His blood tasted better. Richer, headier, more decadent. It had hurt to drink it, even though there had been slightly less burn this time. The experience had been better. Her fangs had finally retracted. She swallowed down, trying to quell her thirst. Ceri turned her back on him and entered the stall. The sooner they got this over and done with, the sooner she could get rid of him. For good! She looked up at the spray, the hot water hitting her face, wetting her hair.

She yelped when he touched the side of her arm. Just a brush of the fingers.

"You don't have to be so jumpy," he said, his voice right behind her. There was a clicking noise as the stall door shut. "Let me help." Despite the hot water, she could still feel his warmth. She could hear his heart beating, the rate elevated and strong.

She held back a sigh as his fingers began to work her back. She could feel the slimy texture of the plant gel. Ceri knew she should tell him to stop. That she could take care of it herself, but his hands felt too good. Her fangs throbbed and her tongue felt like it was sticking to the roof of her mouth. She was tempted to take in a mouthful of water. Unfortunately, it wouldn't help. *Blood!* She'd taken so little from him earlier. A taste really. Enough to whet her appetite but not nearly enough to quench her thirst. She was starving. Her breathing turned choppy, like she'd just run around the block.

"Here." His deep voice enveloped her and goosebumps rose up on her arms. Her already tight nipples hardened some more. It took her a moment to realize he was holding the bowl out to her. "Unless you want me to wash the rest of you as well." His brows arched and the side of his mouth twitched. Why was he being so nice to her when she'd been so bitchy to him?

"I'll do it." She moved out of the spray and took the bowl with shaky hands, hoping he wouldn't notice. Hoping her eyes were normal even if her fangs were not. Long and throbbing.

Oh, good lord!

She watched as Bay stepped under the spray. Watched the water cascade down his skin. His beautiful, warm, sun-kissed skin. He put his head under the stream of water, turning around and leaning back. His cock was still at full alert. Thick and ready. She could hear his heart. Could see a vein throbbing at the base of his neck. Her mouth dropped open. Her teeth, her throat, her—

A low growl left her. Hunger coursed through her. Need like she'd never felt before. She gripped his arm and sank her fangs into his wrist.

Bay growled, his eyes snapping open. She held his gaze as she sucked. So delicious. So amazing.

Pain.

Like before, it hurt to drink from him. Not as much but it still hurt. Her mouth, her throat, her insides were on fire. Like he had lava mixed in with his blood. Her need was greater than her pain though and she sucked again. With a growl, she was forced to pull back after the third mouthful, unable to keep going even though she was still hungry. Not as ravenous as before but nowhere near sated either.

Bay was frowning heavily. His chest heaved. "You need to," he swallowed thickly, his eyes moving down to her chest, which was heaving as well, "stop doing that."

She still had his arm in her grip. "I can't! That's why you need to go." She didn't want him to leave just then. Didn't want anything except him. Didn't care if they were found out. Didn't care about Brant. That they were different species. About feuds and wars and arguments. None of that mattered.

"Go?" He shook his head. "I can't!" he growled. "What are you doing to me?" He gripped her hips. "Tell me to stop."

She couldn't. Ceri shook her head.

"Do it! Tell me." He turned her around, using his knee to open her legs. Her eyes fluttered closed. Her hands were flat against the tiles. He snarled as he thrust into her. Hard. Like he had lost all control in that moment. She loved it. Loved the feeling of his hard cock inside her. Deep inside.

Yes!

She moaned every time he drove into her. "You're addictive," he moaned into her ear. "I can't get enough."

Her feelings exactly.

They were in deep shit. He slowed down, his hands sliding up and down her hips and sides. One moved to cup her breast. Soft grunts left his lips, his hard body was plastered against her back, which was slick from the gel. He kept thrusting into her, slow and easy. *So good!*

She groaned when he kissed her neck. If he nipped her, she was going to come. If his teeth so much as scraped against her. His hands palmed her breasts, tweaked her nipples. She whimpered, pushed back against him with every drive of his cock.

Bay sucked on her earlobe and then…he nipped her there, dragging his teeth along her sensitive flesh.

Her head fell back as her body bowed. Her orgasm was instant and intense, blowing through her like a raging storm. Destroying everything in its wake.

He groaned, clutching her tighter, his body crouching over hers as his movements turned jerky. His thrusts were hard and quick. He groaned again, softer this time as he slowed down, his hips circling. His shaft still drawing out the last of her orgasm.

Ceri was shivering. Vibrating was a better word. Her legs felt weak. Her thirst was back, just as bad as before. This was getting worse. "We shouldn't be doing this," she said with a moan.

"No, we shouldn't," he agreed. His hands circled her, holding her. His chest against her back. He made no move to pull out or to let her go.

"We need to clean up," she said, noticing that the water was no longer as hot as it had been. "We're out of time. I have to make more herb tea for Cooper. Need to."

He pulled out just then, making a noise like it pained him to do so. Bay turned her around, he wiped the water dripping from her forehead and smiled at her. "I'd like to see you again before I go."

"No!" She shook her head, feeling shocked to her core.

"Just to talk."

She looked at him like he'd lost his mind and he chuckled. "Okay, well, maybe to do a little more than talk. Our meeting commences in the morning. I have some free time until then."

"I don't," she countered, shaking her head some more. "I'm nursing a shifter." So much for going out tonight. It had been a bad idea to begin with.

"He will be mostly healed within a few hours. There was no silver involved. Come on!" He took her hand, squeezing. "We need to talk about this."

She was still thirsty. Maybe if she got her fill of him,

she'd be in a better position to get over him. It wasn't true of course. Ceri realized she was talking herself into it. "There is nothing to talk about."

"I think there is, and I think you know it."

"We are attracted to one another and I enjoy drinking your blood." *Understatement of the year.* "It doesn't mean anything. It can't mean anything. End of discussion. Shit!" She noticed that the bowl was on its side on the floor, half the contents had spilled out and was swirling down the drain. She picked it up before more of the gel could run out.

"There is something important I have to ask you and now is not the time or the place. Please." He looked at her with such pleading eyes.

"Fine! Where should we meet?" She shook her head. "Nowhere is safe. This is a crazy idea."

"Nowhere on these actual grounds is safe but maybe we could meet in the wooded area behind the castle. Shall we say ten o'clock?"

"Yes." She nodded, lathering the gel onto herself, concentrating on a particular area the most.

She handed what was left to Bay. "That should be enough. I can make some more if you need it?" Thankfully she'd made too much to begin with.

Bay shook his head. "This will be fine." He got to work as well.

Then she washed quickly, using the shower gel and opened the stall door to leave.

Bay took her wrist. "Tonight at ten. Be there." He used a commanding tone she hadn't heard before. "Don't make me come looking for you, because I will."

She could see he meant it. What was so important that he was willing to risk so much for? Ceri nodded and he let her go.

CHAPTER 12

C eri opened another window. She was tempted to spray some air freshener around her office but that might be too obvious.

"I can't believe you rutted a dragon," Drago chuckled. He'd been laughing his ass off since she'd told him.

"Shut up!" Ceri said. "I don't want anyone finding out. We'd both be in big trouble. It's clear things are still heated between the species." She pointed at the shifter on the bed. She'd given him more tea and finished dressing his wounds, which had already begun to heal. His new skin and eyes would be sensitive for a few days, but he'd be just fine and was already over the worst of it.

"You're right, you do scent…strange, and it is a scent that needs masking." He crinkled his nose. "You say you drank his blood. How was it?"

Divine. Glorious. The best thing she had ever tasted. All of those things – along with *addictive.* Since she couldn't say any of those things she said, "This is no time for chatting. Give me your arm."

Drago did as she said, still grinning. Ceri sank her fangs into his skin. Drago winced. "Easy does it," he groaned.

Her fangs hadn't properly descended and sharpened. *Why?* When the dragon was near, her fangs were so sharp they could slice through freaking steel mesh. Right then, she had very little to work with. Drago deserved the pinch of pain he would have felt. *Asshole!* He was loving this far too much for her liking, when there was nothing to like about this whole sorry situation.

Ceri drank his blood, hoping it would mask the scent of Bay's blood. She would scent a little off for the next day but hopefully not so much that others would know something was up. Ceri shouldn't meet Bay again tonight. She really shouldn't. Firstly, because it would be harder to shake his scent and secondly because she felt like her addiction had worsened. *Not good! Not good at all!* Then thirdly, there was something he wanted to ask her; what could it be? Did the dragon have feelings for her? Was that it? Her heart beat faster at the thought.

Drago's blood was like water to her now. It tasted bland. Like it contained no sustenance. It held zero appeal. She had to force herself to keep drinking.

"I guess that's what happens when you starve yourself of blood and sex. You end up jumping a dragon shifter." Drago chuckled again.

Ceri forced herself to take a few more pulls before letting Drago go. It didn't feel like she'd eaten anything. Then she thought about what he had just said. Drago still didn't know that this wasn't her first encounter with a dragon shifter. With this particular dragon shifter. The only reason she'd had to come clean with him was so that he would let her drink from him before anyone else caught her scent. "Um…I might need more blood first thing tomorrow morning."

Drago frowned. "You shouldn't still be hungry." Then his eyes widened and he choked out a laugh. "Oh, my fuck! You're meeting him again, aren't you?" He chuckled some more, even slapping the side of his leg. "Has someone developed a taste for dragon?" he joked, hitting a nerve, only because it was true.

"Keep your voice down," she whispered, glancing at the sleeping shifter and then at the door. "Those alphas will be here any minute. It's almost been two hours to the minute since I sent them away. They will want to make sure Cooper is okay. Brant might come through as well." She hoped that wasn't the case.

Drago rolled down the sleeve of his shirt, doing up the button on the cuff. "I think it's great. So what? You needed a bit of excitement in your life. Go meet that shifter. Have your way with him." He was grinning. "You can use that plant gel again. It works like a charm. I'll meet you at your place in the morning. I will want to hear all about it."

"Hear all about what?" Brant asked, sauntering into her office like he owned the place.

Ceri cringed inwardly, waiting for Brant's nostrils to flare, waiting for him to explode. It didn't happen.

She pushed out a heavy breath, forcing herself to stay calm.

"Oh, I want to know how things go with the poor shifter," Drago said, still grinning. "I can't believe he got his face fried. He must have said something really offensive to get—"

"This is no laughing matter," Brant growled, narrowing his eyes on Drago. "What are you doing here? Shouldn't you be at training?"

Shit! Now she was getting poor Drago into trouble.

"What, and miss seeing this?' He pointed at the downed male, who looked like a mummy from the chest up, he was swathed in so many bandages.

"You shouldn't have told anyone." Brant turned hard eyes on her.

"I'm sorry. Drago is my best friend." She shrugged. "He called and asked me what I was doing and I told him. Next minute he was here to see for himself."

Brant frowned.

"You," Brant pointed at Drago, "get to training. Not a word to anyone about this."

Drago nodded. "See you in the morning." He winked at her as he left.

"And you," Brant turned to Ceri, "you should have known better. I don't want word of this getting out. I'm hoping there are no more complications. We need to try to heal the rifts, although, there are times when I'm not sure why I bother." He shook his head.

"I won't say anything, I swear," she mumbled.

Just then, the two alphas walked in. The bear still looked pissed. "How is Cooper? He had better be doing well or I'm going to find that dragon—"

"Calm down, Gage." The wolf alpha placed a hand on the other male's chest. "There has been enough violence."

The bear clenched his jaw, he looked like he disagreed. Ceri had a feeling things might get worse before they got better.

She needed to cancel with Bay. It needed to end. There was no way of reaching him though. No safe way. That meant she had to meet him. She'd say what needed to be said and then she was out of there.

No blood.

No sex.

She could be strong. She had to be! There was no other way.

Bay paced back and forth. Maybe she wasn't coming. Maybe he had walked too far into the forest. No, she would be able to scent the path he had taken. Just as he could scent that she hadn't arrived before him. Maybe—

There was a crack of a twig. An almost silent footfall, followed by another. He couldn't believe the level of relief he felt when he saw her approach.

She wore another tiny slip of a dress. He'd noticed that vampire females didn't wear much. They didn't always wear underwear. Never any breast coverings. Ceri was no different. The dress was green. Almost the same vibrant color as her eyes. You could make out her nipples and areolas through the fabric if you really tried, and he did. Did he ever. Like plump ripe peaches tipped with succulent cherries. Ripe for the plucking. Her legs seemed to go on for miles under the short dress. "Don't look at me like that," she whispered, stopping on the other side of the clearing. It was like she was afraid of him. He didn't understand it. It had been the same earlier in her office. From fear and apprehension to jumping him – literally.

"How am I looking at you?" he asked.

"Like you want to eat me." She shivered.

"I do."

Her eyes widened and she drew in a startled breath. Ceri shook her head. "I came to tell you that we can't see each other ever again. You said you wanted to ask me something, so ask and then I'm going."

Bay began walking towards her.

"Um," she stumbled on her words, "I mean it. We can't do this, you should turn and walk away. Go back to your hotel." Again, she looked panicked. It was in her eyes. Her hand went up as if to ward him off.

"What's wrong? You said I could ask you that question.

I came here mainly to talk, just like earlier. There are a few things I need—"

It happened again. Her eyes turned a bright blood red. She made a pained noise. "No!" She shook her head. "Stay back." Her fangs were long and really beautiful. Even in this…altered state, her real vampire form, he assumed…she was gorgeous. Ceri hissed at him, in warning.

Last time this had happened, she'd jumped him and taken blood from him. "Are you thirsty? Is that it?"

Ceri dropped to a crouch and hissed again. Then she nodded. "Yes." Another sob.

"You want my blood?" he asked again. "Why not just," he took a step towards her, holding out his arm in invitation, "take it. I don't mind." Truth was, he wanted her to drink from him. He wanted to rut her again. One last time. Maybe this would be his last chance to rut again ever. And that wasn't him being dramatic. It was the truth.

Then he caught her scent and stopped. "Wait!" It was his turn to hold up his hand, but it didn't help or work. With a low hissing growl, she was on him, her claws in his upper arms and her fangs in his neck. They sank in deep. Pain and pleasure were a heady combination for sure.

Bay groaned as she sucked. Grunted when she sucked a second time. Had to grab his cock and squeeze to keep himself from shooting off when she went in for a third long pull. His balls were so tight, they hurt. She released him with a yell, looking like she was in pain but also in utter rapture. So stunning to behold.

He could scent her arousal. Her pussy would be wet and ready. *What?* He frowned. Now that she was this close and he was able to think – at least somewhat – he could also scent another male on her. His cock throbbed, making it hard to rationalize clearly. The need to fuck drowned everything else out. "Off," he growled. "Take the dress off now." It was that or he would tear it off her.

Ceri pulled the garment over her head, tossing it over a nearby log. By the way she was breathing and the little noises she was making, she was just as desperate as he was. *Good!* The ground was thick with pine needles, moss and dirt. Bay didn't care. "Your knees or your back?" He had to be inside her. It had to happen right then!

Ceri lay down on the ground. Her skin a pure milky white against the dirt. "Open your legs for me." His words were a guttural rasp. He was sure that his scales would be showing because they were rubbing against his skin. A friction that only heightened his need.

Her eyes were still red. Her fangs long. Her breasts slightly swollen, such was her level of arousal. Her pussy was glistening wet. Honeyed nectar. If he hadn't been so mad with need to be inside her, he would have tasted her. He wanted to.

With a growl, he yanked his pants down, stepping out of them. He crouched over her, taking his weight on his arms, feeling her shudder beneath him.

"This is the last time," she groaned, an edge of desperation apparent. "It has to be."

"Yes," he agreed, even though he didn't want it to be the last time. Not by a long shot.

Bay groaned when he plunged inside her welcoming flesh. He took her hard. His knees and hands pressing into the soft, damp soil. The forest filled with the sound of their ragged breathing, of her whimpers and moans.

He didn't want this to end even though he could feel his release fast approaching. Bay wanted to slow down but he couldn't, his body wouldn't let him. Neither would hers. Her pussy sucked him in, holding him, coaxing him. Even his balls slapping against her felt fantastic. His abdominal muscles felt coiled and tight. His eyes large. His body sweaty.

Then she yelled and her pussy closed around him. Squeezing hard. Her heels dug into him as she tightened her legs. Her body went from coaxing to demanding, and he was useless to deny. Bay groaned her name as he came.

She bit down on his shoulder, sucking hard. Bay grit his teeth as he orgasmed all over. A harsh snarl was pulled from him as she sucked a second time. Anybody listening would think they were killing one another. He couldn't keep the noise down.

Her pussy spasmed again as well and she wailed as she let his neck go. The cry turning into a deep groan. It looked like Ceri had the same problem with noise control.

"Shit!" she whispered as soon as she could breathe halfway normally. "Shit!" she said again. "That should never have happened."

"Stop that!" He gripped her chin. "You keep saying that. I wanted it to happen. I hoped it would. I enjoy being inside you. There is no harm in that."

"No harm?" Her eyes filled with tears. "My cousin would be angry. What about your kings? How would they feel?"

"They'd be pissed but screw them, it's not like we plan on mating or anything. It's just sex." He shook his head, "So why does it matter?"

"It's complicating things."

"Not really. We had a good time. We're attracted to one another and have enjoyed each other immensely." Then he caught that scent from earlier. Bay frowned. "Who is this male I keep scenting on you? Is it the same one from before?"

"If I didn't know better, I would say you were jealous."
She pushed on his chest.

Bay chuckled as he pulled out of her welcoming heat
and moved onto his haunches. "I'm not." *He wasn't though,
was he?* That she scented of someone else so soon after
they had rutted irritated him, but it wasn't jealousy.

Ceri sat up, making no move to cover her nakedness.
She had smudges of dirt on her thighs. He was certain
she'd have some on her back as well. "Good, because that
would be...wrong." She shook her head, making a face.
"What did you want to ask?"

"Who is he? You don't scent like you rutted but we
both know that doesn't mean anything."

Her eyes widened. "You really do sound jealous."

"I'm concerned I wasn't able to...ease you sufficiently
that you found the need to go looking for—"

"You can stop right there. I have enjoyed rutting you.
Drago is my friend. That's all he is." She shook her head.
"I needed to try to mask your scent after drinking from
you, that's all."

He couldn't believe the degree of calm he felt. *Good!* So
he was still a decent fuck. It had nothing to do with
jealousy. That would be stupid. Not to mention wrong.

"You wanted to ask me something."

Bay nodded once. He needed to just go ahead and say
it. Just spit it out already. He realized that he felt shame.
He didn't want this beautiful creature to know about his
impotency problems. He didn't want to see a look of pity
in her eyes. To have her never look at him with desire
again.

There was no *again* with her though. Therefore, nothing
to lose. There was only here and now and finding a

possible cure to his problem. If one even existed. He had to try. If he tried and failed, at least he could continue with his head held high. If he didn't at least ask, he would always regret it. He might need to seek her out again and that couldn't happen. Ceri was right about that.

"I'm impotent," he blurted.

CHAPTER 13

*I*mpotent.

Ceri felt confusion wash over her. "What? Sorry. I don't think I heard you correctly."

"No." Bay nodded. "You did. You heard me just fine. I'm impotent."

Ceri frowned and then burst out laughing. She couldn't help it. *Impotent! Really?* It was absurd. Her humor quickly evaporated when he remained perfectly serious. His eyes solemn. The male wasn't joking then.

Come on though. It couldn't be. "If you're impotent, how did we just have sex? How did we have sex all the times before that? You do realize, that's a lot of sex for someone who can't get it up."

"I have no idea how sex with you has been possible." He shook his head. "I was involved in an accident twelve years ago. I'm not going to bore you with the particulars." He was ashamed of how it had happened. "My shaft was completely severed."

"It would have grown back." Ceri glanced down at his cock. "It clearly did grow back."

"The cut was made with a silver blade."

"Oh!" Her eyes widened. "Oh," she repeated, this time with understanding. "Just like with my womb."

"Yes, just like that. My cock grew back but never functioned again. Not until…"

"So, how was sex between us possible?" He could see her mind was running a mile a minute.

"I'm not sure, I was hoping you could tell me. It's clearly related to you drinking from me because every time that happens, my cock gets hard in an instant. The effects quickly wear off though."

The answer to his question was easy. "Drinking, when done between two people who are attracted to one another, is highly sexual. It turns the other person on. The person drinking but mostly the person receiving the bite will be greatly affected. It acts like a major aphrodisiac and I can only assume that that's what happened with you."

He pushed out a breath, looking upset. "Like you pointed out, our species do not get along very well. Sneaking around with willing vampire females – if I can find one, that is – isn't my idea of a long-term plan." He shook his head.

Hearing him talk of rutting other females – particularly of her species – made her feel uncomfortable. So that was why he had come back to see her, so that he could try to cure himself. Not for her. It had nothing to do with seeing her again. Of course he wasn't interested in her in that way. She was a lay to him. Ceri snorted internally. It should have made her feel relieved. Happy even.

The only thing it made her feel though was angry. Angry at herself for even thinking such a thing. Angry for caring and then really pissed at him for being just another asshole. It was disappointing.

It turned out that despite seeming kind and sweet, Bay was just like the vampire males, ready to use her for their own pleasures and then take up with a human so that they could have young. She wasn't ever worth more than a good rutting.

"Are you okay? Your eyes are turning red all over again. Do you need more blood? More sex?" He grinned, making her blood boil. "I would be happy to give you both." She was appalled to find her body respond. Her nipples had stiffened. Need tightened her belly.

It all just pissed her off a whole lot more that she wanted him so much, even after he admitted to using her. "I know exactly what you need."

"I'll bet you do." His eyes brightened. He sat on his ass, legs splayed. Abs taut, shoulders wide. His smile taunting and beautiful. Her eyeballs didn't seem to care that he was a using bastard. Neither did the rest of her body.

There was only one 'cure' she could think of. Ceri shouldn't help him. He didn't deserve it. Thing was, she knew what it felt like to feel like half a person. To have a part of you stripped away. She would never be a mother. Chances were good she'd never find love because if it. What species' male wanted a female incapable of bearing young?

None.

None she knew of anyway. Bay included. He wanted to be cured and he wanted to be on his way. Ceri straddled him, sinking down on his cock.

Bay's eyes narrowed onto hers. They brightened up with intense heat as she ground down. He groaned as she got down to the hilt, completely joined. Then she began to work his cock, up and down. His jaw tensed and he gripped her hips. Bay leaned forward and tried to kiss her, but she turned her head away. This wasn't about enjoyment, about drawing out the moment. This was a means to an end. It was fucking. She sank her fangs into his neck and sucked his blood. Bay immediately tensed, she heard his heart stop for a second. Heard the air stick in his lungs. Then he snarled and she felt heat deep inside as he ejaculated. She sucked again and his snarl turned into a hard groan, his body shuddering beneath her. Heat flooded her body, her pussy tightened but she held off her own release, continuing to ride him. The third pull was almost too much to bear, but this time she managed a fourth before her insides felt like they were burning up. She let him go, even though she was loath to do so.

Next, she bit into her own wrist, still grinding on his cock shamelessly. "You drink from me," she moaned each word, absurdly close to coming.

His eyes narrowed. "What?" he growled. "Why?"

"You want a cure, then drink," she urged. "Before I heal." It wouldn't take long for that to happen. "Drink!" she demanded. "Now!"

Bay kept his eyes locked with hers as he closed his mouth over the wound she had made on her arm and sucked.

A keening noise left her as pleasure flooded her system. Her pussy spasmed so hard she was sure she might hurt him.

Instead, he growled, his eyes rolling back. He gripped her arm with both his hands and sucked again, harder this time. Her back bowed and she yelled his name. He sucked again and she saw stars. Then he was gripping her hips and jerking into her, grunting loudly as he came again.

She'd never had frantic out of control sex like this before. It was as beautiful as it was ugly. This was how she always imagined it to be between lovers. Between mates. Something special and rare. Only it wasn't that. Not at all.

It felt like a slap in the face. Like a cold bucket of water.

Ceri pulled away. She'd never felt lonelier. She stood up and took a few stumbling steps in the opposite direction, picking up her discarded dress and purse. "Here." She tossed a bottle of the gel at him. It landed on the ground next to him. "No-one must know." Ceri turned to walk away.

"Wait," he growled.

Ceri paused, not turning back.

"Is that it?" he asked. "Am I cured?"

A single tear tracked down her cheek. She ignored it, ignored him and walked away.

CHAPTER 14

The next day…

"And?" Drago sniffed the air as soon as he opened the door. "Somebody got some." He grinned as he stepped to the side to let her in. "You smell weird again, like you were smoking or something." He sniffed again. "Cigars rather than cigarettes." He wrinkled his nose and then widened his eyes. "You weren't smoking, were you? You did actually get laid again?" Then he grinned because he knew the answer to his own question.

Ceri didn't want to talk about it but Drago would be like a dog after a bone if she didn't give him something. "Yes, we rutted again. I definitely wasn't smoking anything. He leaves in a couple of hours, so that's the end of that." Hopefully Drago would drop the whole thing.

She should have known better than to think he would. He scrutinized her. "You aren't glowing, or on a high, or happy or anything. You seem…down." He cocked his head slightly, really giving her the once-over. "Why are you down? What happened?"

"Not at all." She waved her hand and walked further into his apartment. "Oh good, you have coffee brewing."

"Don't try to change the subject." She turned to Drago,

who folded his arms. "Why aren't you on a sex high? Was the rutting not up to scratch?" He made a face. "Was the dragon crap? I thought he was good? Why else would you go back for seconds?"

"The sex was good. More than good actually."

"Why are you so down then?"

She helped herself to a coffee cup and sighed softly. "I don't want to talk about it." Ceri knew it was the worst thing she could say because Drago wouldn't let it go now.

"You'll feel better if you talk about it. I guarantee it. Are you sad he's leaving?" His eyes lit up. "Are you in love with this male?"

"No!" she replied. "Not at all. Don't be crazy." Ceri poured herself some of the steaming brew. "Why does that make you happy, at any rate? It would be terrible if I had fallen in love with a dragon."

He shrugged. "It would be interesting."

"Me, being in love with someone I could never have, is not interesting, that would be awful."

"I suppose. You say it isn't that, what is it then? I'll have a cup too." He pointed at her coffee and leaned against the counter, his eyes on her.

"He was using me," she blurted.

Drago burst out laughing. "Of course he was, just like you were using him. Wait a minute! Why would you care about a thing like that? You must have feelings for this dragon. Otherwise, you wouldn't be so upset about this."

"I don't have feelings for him, it's just…" She pushed out a heavy breath. Drago already knew so much, what did it matter if she told him all of it. She reached into the cupboard and pulled out another cup.

"Just what?"

She huffed out a breath. "I didn't meet Bay yesterday."

Drago's frown deepened. "What are you talking about?"

"You know when I went to Beachhaven on vacation?"

"Yes." Drago nodded once, a grin beginning to spread across his handsome face. "Don't tell me you guys… Did you…?"

She rolled her eyes and nodded once. "Yes, we spent the night together then as well. Just one night. I checked out before morning. We didn't talk much."

"I'll bet."

"I didn't think I'd ever see him again and…" She raised her brows.

"And then he shows up here." Drago laughed. "That's bizarre. So yesterday was the second time you saw him and last night the third."

She nodded. "He brought the shifter in and then came back to talk to me, only…" Ceri told him what had happened. Keeping it brief and sticking to the facts. "So you'll excuse me for feeling a little down about the whole thing. I guess I don't feel good enough." She felt her lip wobble and chewed down on it. "I don't think I'll ever find someone willing to give me a chance. Willing to be with me even though I can't have kids." She swallowed down a lump of emotion clogging her throat.

"Hey, that's bullshit." Drago went over to her and folded her up in a hug. "You have me. You'll always have me."

"You know I love you a crazy amount, but I'm kind of looking for more than friendship." She gave him a squeeze. "I appreciate what we have. Don't misunderstand me."

"You want more." He pulled away, pretending to be hurt. "You have my heart and soul, which is more than any other female ever had, what more could you possibly want?" She could tell he was teasing.

"Someone to wake up to every morning and, um, I don't know, sex, regular, really hot sex." Like the kind she'd had with Bay.

"Now that can be arranged. You know I would be willing to—Ouch!" He yelped when she hit him on the arm. "I'm only kidding. Sex would ruin things between us." He chuckled, his big body vibrated.

"Sex with you would be lousy."

"What?" He sucked in a breath, clutching a hand to his chest. "How can you say such a thing? Talk about bruising a male's ego."

"Because we have zero chemistry. Less than zero." She shook her head.

"Yeah, I've never understood that. You are quite literally the only female who has never shown any attraction to me. I don't understand it."

It was her turn to scrutinize him. Her turn to laugh. "I watched you eat your boogers in first grade. There is no going back from that."

Drago chuckled, his face turning pink. "I was six years old. It was a phase and it didn't last."

"The mental picture is still up here." She pointed at her skull.

"Okay," he took her hand, turning serious, "so you're not in love with this male. I get why you're upset. You need to know that one day, a male will come along and he will love you no matter what. He will fall for you because you are amazing, and so worth it, and if it weren't for those boogers I ate in first grade we'd probably be mated right now." He grinned.

She choked out a laugh and shook her head.

"In all seriousness, it will happen and when it does, you'll know it's true love. It won't just be some asshole male settling because you are fertile. It will be real love. The deep and meaningful kind you crave, and until then, I am here for you."

"Only until then?" She smiled.

Drago rolled his eyes. "No, dufus, for always. We are friends for forever."

"Good and with that in mind, please feed me." She actually felt a little queasy at the thought of drinking from him. Ceri had to though. There was no other choice. It had been a long, restless night. She wasn't feeling herself. Things would improve. All would be well. She'd get over whatever this was with Bay and move on. The sooner that happened the better.

"So," Brant said, smoothing his jacket. "Things to look out for. The hunters may disguise themselves as military personnel. They own a fleet of ex-army helicopters." He went on to describe makes and models. In truth, Bay struggled to concentrate on what was being said.

They were leaving straight after this final wrap-up. It didn't feel like much had been achieved. He'd tried to go back to see Ceri but had almost been caught by Torrent. He'd lied and said he was out for a walk.

All he wanted to do was fix things between them. He didn't like that they had walked away from each other as enemies. Ceri didn't feel like an enemy. Not even close.

The male hadn't completely believed him and it might be his imagination but it seemed like Torrent had been keeping an eye on him ever since.

That he had been diverted was probably for the best

anyway. He'd almost made a fool of himself. It was clear the vampire wanted nothing more to do with him.

He wasn't sure if drinking her blood had cured him. He didn't think so – not that he'd tried to disprove it yet. Yesterday had been jam-packed and had included a dinner which ended late. Team-building had started at seven this morning. They were leaving in a few minutes.

"The actual hunters themselves," Brant said, while looking directly at him, probably sensing his mind had wandered, "come from old money. At least ninety-nine percent of them. The other one percent used to come from money but lost their fortunes somewhere along the line."

"Fortunes that were never theirs," Torrent mumbled.

"What was that?" Brant looked at his king. "Did you want to add something?"

Torrent shook his head. "No. Just that these hunters steal from those they assassinate. We're talking mass genocide here, followed by mass pillaging."

"They are without honor. Your females and children would be murdered just as readily as your males," Blaze said. "I do not believe that they will be satisfied with slaughtering our species. They live for death and destruction. None of you are safe."

"Be on the look-out for anyone with a tattoo on their left hand. The top." He pointed at that part on his own hand. "It would be a plain, black ink of the all-seeing eye." Brant pushed a device in his hand and a picture appeared on the white screen of the tattoo in question. "We have each other's contact details. Let's report any sightings. Any strange happenings. Let's work together to eradicate this scourge."

"We plan on taking a much harsher approach. Any

helicopters found to be in our territory, where we can prove without a doubt are hunters," *A difficult task.* "will be taken out," Blaze announced. "Each of our tribes has a Head of Defense. Going forward, this individual will be given a new title." Blaze turned to him. "From now on you will be known as Head of War. We are no longer going to sit by. We are fighting back." He pounded the table. The wood creaked.

Bay nodded once, feeling the weight of what would be expected of him. In truth, he had never been much of a fighter. Sure, he *could* fight. He'd always had a knack for combat, but he didn't revel in it like many of the others. Like Flood. The male was much better suited to the role. Even Beck would be a better candidate. He swallowed hard.

CHAPTER 15

Two months and three weeks later…

"I'm thirsty all the time. My breasts have grown. At least," Lily unbuttoned her blouse and opened it, exposing her chest, "I think they have."

Ceri's eyes were drawn to the female's boobs. "I'm sorry." She made a face. "I've never seen your breasts before, so I have no idea if they are bigger or not." She shrugged. "Your nipples are dark though. That could be a sign."

"They feel achy and tender at times, tingly at others." Lily cupped her breasts, giving them a squeeze.

"It is very early days yet." Ceri smiled. New life was to be celebrated. She hoped with all her might that Lily was indeed with child, seeing that this female was one of the few with a pelvis wide enough to birth an infant. "We will know soon enough. You will be able to take a pregnancy test at about six weeks."

"Those aren't always accurate when it comes to vampire pregnancies though?"

"I'm afraid not. You get false negatives but never false positives. You might be lucky enough to get a positive early on. Then you'll know for sure."

Lily frowned. "I hope so. Otherwise, I will have to wait three months before a heartbeat can be detected."

"Yes, that's the other surefire way to know. I'm sorry," Ceri added when she saw Lily's frown. She felt sympathy for the other female. "Vampire young grow very slowly for those first few months and then very rapidly for the last few. You will have to wait between twelve and fifteen weeks before a heartbeat can be detected. Females have reported nausea, heightened appetite, strange cravings. You may have spotting at around five to six weeks. That is the fetus nestling into your womb lining. Then there's fatigue, mood swings and possible headaches. The biggest giveaway is that you won't have your menstruation, but— "

Lily moaned. "Not another 'but.'"

Ceri nodded. "Unfortunately, this isn't an exact science. Symptoms can vary from female to female. Some females continue to have their menstruation throughout the pregnancy. Mostly though, your menstruation will stop or become very light." She pulled in a deep breath, suddenly realizing she hadn't had her own menstruation in a while. The last one was much less than normal. How long had it been? Too long? It was a pain in the ass that she still got her monthly bleeds even though she couldn't actually become pregnant. All of the hassle and none of the rewards.

"Did you hear what I said?" Lily asked.

Pull it together, Ceri. "No, sorry, please repeat the question." She forced herself to smile.

"I said what about instinct? Stuart and I have been trying for almost a year and this is the first time I actually feel pregnant. I can't explain it, I just do." She put a hand to her belly.

"Some females have reported having this instinct you talk of, where others have been completely clueless." She reached forward and squeezed Lily's arm. "I really hope you are with child. I couldn't think of nicer people. You and Stuart love each other so much. You're going to make fantastic parents."

Lily beamed. She nodded.

"Try not to feel too disappointed if you're not with child though. You guys can keep trying. Vampire females don't become pregnant easily, but it will happen. You need to stay positive."

"I will." Lily smiled. The female stood up. "Thank you for listening and for being so supportive. It's such a pity you can't have young, you would've made a wonderful mom."

Ceri felt that familiar squeezing inside her chest. She smiled at Lily. "Let me know as soon as you hear anything either way." She didn't want to be pessimistic, but she also didn't want the female getting her hopes up just to be dashed.

"I will." They said their goodbyes and Lily left.

Ceri glanced at the clock on the wall. Best she hurry, she was meeting Drago for lunch. Ceri straightened up her desk and hung her lab coat on the hook at her door before heading out. She was meeting him in the gardens. They often had a picnic-style lunch on one of the benches overlooking the lake.

It was nice to get outdoors. She didn't get out enough, always stuck between the four walls of her office. Drago was already there, already waiting for her.

His eyes lit up as soon as he saw her. He was holding a paper bag on his lap. Her mouth watered at what she hoped was inside. "Did you make me one?" she asked, eyeing the bag.

"Did you bring a vein?" He narrowed his eyes, glancing down at her wrist.

She narrowed her eyes back at him. "What do you think?"

"I'm starving." His gaze was still locked on her wrist.

"But you drank yesterday." Then she realized something. "Wait a minute, you said you took a female home last night, didn't you drink from her?"

Drago looked sulky. "I tried to drink from her, but I much prefer your blood. I've developed a serious taste for it. Now, I'm really hungry, like super hungry." His irises looked red-tinged. They shouldn't be. Only if he was starving would his eyes be that color. Drago wasn't starving, or angry or turned on.

Ceri held out her arm and watched as he sank his fangs into her and drank. Drago groaned as he swallowed his first gulp and groaned some more on the next pull. The groans were followed by loud gulping swallows. "Um, that's enough," she said after about a minute. Then she tried to pull her hand away. "Drago," she said in a stern voice.

He seemed to suck even harder. There was another pinch. Instead of stopping as she asked, he was making a second set of holes in her skin.

"Drago stop!" she urged, trying to pull her arm away. "Stop!" This time she shouted.

Nothing.

Well, not nothing, he sucked again. He ignored her flat out. Ceri whacked him on the side of the head. Hard. Drago finally let go, clutching a hand to the side of his face. "Hey, what was that for? I was about to let go." The sheepish look on his face told her that he probably wasn't.

"What the hell was that?" Her voice was stern.

"I'm sorry! I don't know what came over me."

"No, really, what's going on with you?"

He shrugged. "I've always enjoyed a wide variety of blood types. A wide variety of veins in general." He cast his gaze over the lake. Two pairs of swans floated on the crystal surface. Yellow beaks, curved necks, white plumes. Majestic and beautiful.

"What you're trying to say is that you're a male slut?" She smiled.

He shook his head for a moment or two before nodding. "Yes, that's exactly what I'm saying." He chuckled.

She did too. "What was that then? It was like you couldn't stop there for a moment."

"I don't know!" He sounded frustrated. Even raked a hand through his hair. "Lately, I've only wanted to drink your blood. I don't enjoy other females anymore. I've tried with four others just in this last week. Their blood tastes flat to me." He shook his head. "Completely flavorless, almost like I'm drinking…" He shrugged like he was unable to come up with the right word.

"Water."

"Yes, exactly. Their blood doesn't sate me, not in the way yours does." Just like she had felt about Bay. She had struggled after he left. Things had improved day by day. Little by little.

Then Drago looked at her funny, cocking his head. "You are one to talk though."

Ceri frowned. "What do you mean?"

"You have the opposite problem. You haven't had anything to drink in almost two weeks."

She snorted out a laugh. "Rubbish. That can't be true

or I'd be freaking out – fangs, red irises and all. I'd have attacked someone long ago."

"It's been two weeks. I assumed you were getting blood from someone else." He looked at her funny. Like she had just grown a third eye in the middle of her forehead or something. "You *are* getting blood elsewhere aren't you?"

She shook her head. "No, but you must have your timeline wrong. I drank from you just the other day."

"Those two or three sips hardly count as drinking."

"Of course they count, and it was more than two or three sips." It had been, hadn't it? Yes, it had, why was she even second-guessing it? "Did you bring the sandwich?"

"Yes, yes!" he pretended to sound bored. "Ham and mustard on fresh white bread."

She nodded, positively salivating at the thought of sinking her fangs into the sandwich. "Please tell me you put a good couple of layers of ham on there?"

"I laid the ham on thick."

"Good!" she groaned. "And what about the pickles? You put pickles—"

"Yes! I put a couple of pickle slices on there was well."

"Thank you so much." Ceri hugged him. "Now hand over the food," she said as soon as she released him.

He handed her the bag, which she made quick work of. "What about you?"

"I already ate." He winked at her.

She unwrapped the grease-proof paper and sank her teeth into all that was delicious in this world. Moaning around her food as she chewed.

"Vampires aren't supposed to enjoy solids that much." Drago looked disgusted.

"Says the male who has developed bloodlust but only for his best friend's blood." She took another bite and closed her eyes, savoring the taste.

"Do you still think about him?" Drago asked.

"Who?" Ceri knew exactly who he was referring to.

"The dragon. Do you think of him? Miss him?"

"Why do you ask?" She didn't want to talk about this.

"You haven't been anywhere near other males. It's not healthy. I was wondering if it had something to do with the dragon."

It had everything to do with Bay. She had made progress though. Serious progress. She didn't crave his blood anymore. Not like she used to, but she did think about him often. Several times a day. "I sometimes think about him," she played it down. "I wonder what he's doing."

"Do you think your blood cured him?"

Most days she hoped it had. She had the odd selfish day where she hoped it hadn't. The thought of Bay with other females didn't sit right with her. It made her feel jealous. It made her feel sad. It made her long for something that she could never have, was stupid to even think about. "I don't know. I hope for him that it did."

"I don't think so. Vampire blood has healing qualities but only on a fresh injury."

She shrugged. "It was the only thing I could think of. You never know…drinking from him did the trick when it shouldn't have." She took another bite of her sandwich, noticing that there wasn't much left. "You didn't make me two, did you?" Ceri looked back in the bag, finding it empty. Then she made a sad face at Drago.

Drago shook his head. "And on that note, there's something I've been meaning to tell you, as a friend."

Ceri quickly swallowed down her mouthful of food. "That sounds ominous."

Drago shook his head again. "It's nothing bad. Nothing terrible."

"Okay, now you're making me worried. What is it?"

"You know I think you're gorgeous right?" He raised his brows.

"Yes," she sounded skeptical. How could she not?

"Well, you've been eating a ton of food lately. Like, every time I look at you, you're eating and it's starting to…well…it's—"

"Are you trying to tell me I'm fat?" Her clothing *had* been feeling tight of late.

"Not fat, no. Just," he shook his head, "you're bigger than you were. All of this eating isn't healthy. Your food choices also leave a lot to be desired. Sandwiches," he pointed at the half-eaten one in her hands, "red velvet cupcakes, steaks the size of my face."

It was all true! Eating made her feel better. Eating had helped her with her dragon blood cravings. It had become a 'thing.' Her thing. Her clothing was tight. Most of her jeans didn't fit anymore. There were one or two dresses and other items that had followed suit. Her boobs had started to bounce when she did anything other than walk. They bounced and juggled so badly that she had started to think of wearing a bra. She sighed. "I have been using food as a crutch." She nodded, looking at the swans as they glided across the lake in pairs. "The whole thing with Bay made me a bit depressed. That, and lonely. I've never felt so alone. Food helps ease that. I'll go on one of those human diets. I'll talk to Tanya about it. Although I don't want to bother her, seeing as she's due to have her baby in the next couple of weeks."

"Google healthy eating then. I'm not trying to be nasty or anything. It's just something you need to be aware of. I happen to think you look amazing." His gaze slid to her breasts.

"You are not checking me out."

He cleared his throat and sat up straighter. "Of course not!" he said too quickly. "What I'm trying to say is that you are gorgeous and have become curvy and even sexier, but all this eating isn't healthy."

Drago had to work hard to keep his physique in top form. He was meticulous about what he ate, so it was only natural that he would notice and say something to her. Then he grinned. "I'm sure it's all the food that's making your blood taste so good. Once you're on that human diet thing, I won't crave it as much."

"I'm sure you're right." She took another bite of her sandwich.

"Hey, I thought you were going to go easy on those."

"I will." She nodded. "After this." The grease-paper crinkled as she held up what was left of the meal. "I'll talk to Tanya or Google a healthy eating plan. I'll figure something out and start the diet tomorrow."

CHAPTER 16

His eyes stung from the constant searching. His wings felt fatigued from flying. Bay and his team had been at it for hours. He signaled to the others in his formation with a gruff bark. It was time to descend. To take a much-needed break. Bay headed to the outcrop of trees. They could shelter there. He turned to the right as they slowly descended, watching the sun as it glinted off the ocean. To the left, rolling hills became majestic mountains.

They touched down and shifted. Cracking noises filled the air. They were all breathing hard. Beck had a sheen of sweat on his brow. Bay took a minute to compose himself, watching as the others moved to shady spots. They sat or even lay down. "I can see why you raised this issue. You were right," Bay addressed Beck. "Twelve-hour shifts are too long. We will have to find another way to get the coverage we need."

Beck nodded. "By the end of the day, the males are exhausted. What if we were to happen upon those hunters at that point? We would not be in a position to take them on, let alone flee."

Bay nodded. They were actively searching for the hunters. They'd taken down two choppers in the last three months. One had unfortunately escaped, killing one of the

Fire males and injuring three more. Sightings since then had become rare. The dragons were not complacent enough to believe that this was over though. It wasn't. The hunters were regrouping. They had to do the same.

"Yes, but how do we keep regular eyes on all sections of our territory? We don't have enough males." Bay shook his head, feeling frustrated.

"I've been thinking about that," Beck said. "They use technology, why don't we do the same?"

"I'm listening." Bay folded his arms.

"We can use satellite-based tracking tech, as well as radar. All of the tribes would need to be on board, but we could technically monitor our borders using technology rather than running constant teams. The satellite technology is still in its testing phase, so I suggest we start with radar since it's tried and tested." He pulled in a deep breath. "I can draw up a report of the pros and cons. I'm not saying that we wouldn't have to run teams at all, but we would need significantly less manpower than our current situation calls for."

"Sounds good. Yes, I would like a report. I'll do some research of my own as well. I'll need a strong case to present to Torrent and then to Blaze in turn. I think you're onto something though."

"I just wanted to say that I think it's great that you made the call to come out today. Most males in leadership positions wouldn't lower themselves to come on a scouting run."

Bay shrugged. "I am not most males. I must say though that I ask myself often what Flood would do, or how Flood would handle a situation. I am glad that he has at least been allowed to come back."

"As a team leader." Beck shook his head. "It is killing

him. I wonder how long Torrent is going to make him suffer?"

"Probably until I fuck up."

"Don't be so hard on yourself, you are doing a good job." Beck stretched his back. "Let's sit for a while. We will need to leave soon and I'm tired."

"We all are." Bay took a seat on a log. Beck chose a grassy spot at the base, using the log as a backrest. "You are working too hard. You need to get out." His friend smiled. There was this glint to his eyes that Bay knew well.

"What is it? What are you concocting? Whatever it is, I'm not interested. I have too much going on to—"

"You were unwillingly celibate for years. You now have a cock that actually works and all you have done with it for three months is whack off – and not even that often. We dragons have a fantastic sense of smell, so don't even try to deny it."

Bay thrust a hand through his hair, which he noted needed a cut. He pushed out a sigh. "You shouldn't be sniffing around in my business."

"Can't help it. What's going on with you?"

"We spoke about this," Bay countered, not wanting to go down this road.

"Yes, and you told me you were going to get some. Our females would be all over you, fresh meat in a high-powered position. You might even be able to win yourself one of the last remaining fertile females, but no, you're not interested."

"Of course I am," he lied. Truth was, none of them held any appeal. He knew the rutting would be subpar after being with the vampire. After Ceri. What was the point? "I'm busy. Far too busy to be chasing skirt."

"A male can never be too busy for pussy."

Bay didn't say anything.

"What, you don't believe me?"

Of course Bay believed Beck because it was true, but he couldn't say so, now could he?

"All I can say is if I were in your shoes, I would've headed into town for a week of non-stop rutting. Delta," Beck called to one of the males further away. He was lounging under a huge oak.

"Yes." The male began to rise to his feet.

"Stay where you are." Beck held up a hand. "I see you're on the list for the Stag Run next week, are you going?"

The male's eyes lit up. "Yes, of course. I wouldn't miss it for anything."

"What about you, Morgan?"

The male groaned. "I am absolutely going. You would have to throw me in a silver cage and knock me out cold to keep me from heading out." Then he looked panicked. "You're not canceling, are you? Please tell me you aren't canceling?"

"Well," Beck shrugged, looking pained, "our leader has said that he is too busy to attend. The threat of those hunters still looms. Our lair is at risk. I am indeed thinking of canceling. If Bay refuses to go then," he shrugged again, "I might just have to. That goes for all Stag Runs going forward."

The males looked crestfallen. Several looked like they might cry, this despite being hardened warriors. A couple of them began talking and grumbling amongst themselves.

"No," Bay stood up, "I will attend, as will all of you. It is important for all of us to unwind." The males went nuts. Whooping and leaping. The joy on their faces was almost contagious. Almost. He turned to Beck and whispered under his breath, "Bastard."

Beck laughed. "It's going to be fun! You are going to get yourself laid once and for all. It's time you got over that vampire female," he whispered the last under his breath. "She helped you. You were highly compatible, I'm assuming, but pining over something that can never be won't get you anywhere."

The male was right. He nodded once. "I said I would attend and I will."

"Good." Beck tapped him good-naturedly on the side of the arm.

It was time he moved on. Beck was right. He might think of Ceri often, but he knew for sure that the female didn't feel the same. She had left without so much as a backward glance. It was over. Not that there had been anything in the first place. He needed to remember that!

CHAPTER 17

A week later...

C eri stopped walking, she put both hands to the small of her back and pushed. It had been a long day, many hours of it spent on her feet. A difficult day.

One abortion. One womb removal surgery. Humans called it a hysterectomy. Drugs didn't work on vampires. Not like they did on humans. The procedures were agonizing. Ceri had experienced one of them herself. She knew exactly how it felt to have your skin sliced open with a silver blade. To have a piece of your body stripped away. A piece of your soul along with it. She hoped that Angelique didn't live to regret her decision. Both females were young. Thankfully, they were both doing well.

The sun was already setting by the time she made it to her apartment. Her feet ached as well. The only thing she could think of was a nice bubble bath, followed by dinner and bed. Ceri yawned, putting her purse on the coffee table. She kicked off her shoes and went through to the bathroom where she started the bath, pouring a good helping of lavender-scented bubble bath into the tub. She watched the water swirl and bubbles begin to form.

Then she went to the kitchen and turned on the oven.

Ceri placed her dinner in the center of the oven rack. It would take at least an hour to cook. She poured herself a large glass of chilled orange juice before heading back to the bathroom. She set the juice on the floor next to the bath, where she could reach it easily. She grabbed the paperback thriller she was trying to get through, placing it next to the glass, along with a towel. Then she undressed, making quick work of her summer dress. It was floral and tight-fitting on account that her diet wasn't working. Maybe it was because she wasn't strictly following the eating plan Tanya had given her. She was just too hungry. Craved too many things. Things like steak and pie and cake and ham sandwiches. *Oh, those ham sandwiches.*

Tomorrow was another day. She was having chicken pot pie for dinner with all the trimmings and then she would think of dieting again in the morning. She couldn't let her lovely dinner go to waste. Anyway, Ceri liked the fuller-figured her. Other females had begun to notice. They'd asked her what she was doing. How had she managed to get her hips fuller, curvier and her breasts so much plumper. She'd told them to eat more, much more. Several females were on the 'reverse diet' – so to speak.

Ceri lowered herself into the water, stretching out. She sighed with contentment as she felt her muscles relax. That was so much better. So much more—

She sat up so quickly that some of the water sloshed over the side of the tub. Ceri was breathing heavily. She had a hand on the lower part of her belly. A reaction. *What the hell?* What was that?

She'd had a bit of a rumbly tummy the last few days but that was something else. It felt like something moved. Like something…kicked. *No!* She was imagining things that simply were not there.

Ceri sucked in a few deep breaths and lay back down. She forced herself to breathe normally. To clear her head. To relax. She had a bit of indigestion. That's all it was. It had to be. She even smiled at herself for being such an overreacting idiot.

Then it happened again.

Harder this time. A soft thumping feeling. A tapping. There…there it was again, slightly to the right this time. She could hardly breathe. Her eyes felt wide in her head. Her hand moved to her belly, closing over the spot. *There!* Another soft thump. She couldn't feel it inside. It wasn't hard enough to feel with her hand even though she pressed down. There were a few more taps and thumps and then nothing.

She could hear her ragged breathing in the small space of the bathroom. Ceri didn't know what to think. It felt like she had something inside her. What could she possibly have inside her? One answer kept coming back, only it wasn't possible. She couldn't be pregnant. She'd undergone surgery to prevent it from happening. An irreversible surgery. It wasn't possible.

Ceri got out of the bath and toweled herself off. She stood in front of the mirror, like she often did. Only this time she looked. She really looked. Her breasts were much bigger than they had been. Her nipples seemed plumper and darker. Was it just her imagination that they were darker? She didn't think so.

She looked herself over, standing to the side. Then she ran into the living room and called Drago.

Thankfully he picked up after two rings. A female giggled in the background. "What's up?" he asked, sounding concerned.

There was a murmuring. "Not now," he spoke away

from the phone. "Are you okay?" he asked, speaking into the receiver. "You haven't called me this late, out of the blue, for a very long time."

"It's not late."

"It is for you, grandma."

She wanted to smile at his joke, but she couldn't. "I need to see you," she blurted. "Right now, and no, it can't wait. I can hear I'm interrupting and—"

"I'll be there in five minutes," Drago said. Ceri could hear whoever he was with protesting as he put down the phone.

Ceri toweled off her hair and quickly got dressed, choosing a pair of yoga pants and a t-shirt. Then she began pacing. Drago was there four minutes later.

He knocked and came in. "Are you okay?"

"I am...I think."

"What do you mean you think?" He frowned. "Speak to me."

"I'm sorry I ruined your plans for the night."

Drago made a face. "I wasn't into her. I haven't been into any of them of late," he mumbled. "Enough about me. This is about you. Spill."

"You're going to think I'm crazy." She paced away from him. "*I* think I'm crazy for even thinking this, but I don't know what else to think."

"Tell me what's going on and we can discuss it. I can see you're freaked out."

She nodded. "I am. Big time. I felt something...something inside me."

"What?" Drago frowned. "I'm not sure what you mean."

"Movement inside my stomach."

Drago made a face. "Okay, you're losing me here."

"Kicking. I felt definite kicking inside my belly. This belly." She lifted her shirt to just below her breasts. Then she stood to the side.

"I told you to knock it off with all the bad food." He shook his head. "The burgers and fries. I saw you with a whole box of donuts on Tuesday. Now look, you've got indigestion and you've put on more weight."

"My breasts are huge."

"A definite bonus for sure." Drago nodded. "I think you look amazing. Very sexy, but I can't agree because it isn't healthy. You aren't drinking enough either. Don't make me start on you about that."

"Actually. I think it might be related. The not feeling much like drinking, my weight gain, my boobs, the kicking." She put a hand to her stomach. "I went through a patch where I was really nauseous. I put it down to wanting Bay's blood. You remember how much weight I lost. How sick I felt."

He nodded. "You said you were addicted to drinking from the male, but that's not true."

"My blood has changed. I think it might have. It might be why you can't get enough of my blood."

He licked his lips, his eyes moving to her pulse. "You see?" she said. "Just talking about drinking from me is making you thirsty."

"Come on, it can't be."

"No," she shook her head, "I agree. It can't possibly be. There is only one way to find out for sure though. I need to rule it out so that I can move on."

The seatbelt bit into her shoulder as the vehicle hit a pothole. "Slow down."

"Sorry." Drago took his foot off the gas a little. "I guess I'm freaking out a bit too. I mean, what if you are...you know?"

"Pregnant." She felt her heart beat faster. Felt panic rise.

"Yes." Drago nodded. "That wouldn't be good, would it?"

"No, I don't think so, although, I don't know. Vampires can have shifter young, even those of us with narrow hips. But the shifters I'm referring to are bears, wolves and panthers, not dragons. We don't have much information about the dragons. All I know is that it's too soon to be feeling kicking."

"Unless you became pregnant on the Beachhaven trip, then you would be much further along. Your pregnancy would be more in tune with a vampire pregnancy, which is bad."

"Very bad." She swallowed hard. "Either way, it's too late to terminate."

"You're on the cusp. You could still do it. You should still." Drago's hands tightened on the wheel.

"We don't even know that I'm...pregnant yet."

The vehicle hit the smooth surface of tar. "We will in five minutes."

"Pity I ran out of pregnancy tests. I don't keep very many on account of not many of our females becoming pregnant."

"You have been a bit forgetful lately. Is that a symptom as well?" Drago glanced her way before looking back at the road.

"Yes, I suppose it is. Are you sure there's a twenty-four-hour drugstore in Sweetwater?"

Drago nodded. "Yes. They have a big neon sign."

"Classy."

"Very." He turned and smiled at her. "This is going to be okay."

She nodded once, shoving more panic aside. It was no use jumping to conclusions. Not yet.

Drago insisted on going in while she waited in the car. Five minutes later he walked out carrying a bag which he handed to her as he slipped behind the wheel. She looked inside and burst out laughing. "Really? Six tests? You bought six?"

He shrugged. "Better safe than sorry, and we're not waiting to get back either."

Two minutes later they pulled into a gas station.

"Do you want me to come in with you?" Drago asked.

"You want to watch me pee on a stick?"

"I won't look."

Ceri smiled and shook her head. "I can manage."

He nodded. "I'm sure there's some logical explanation."

"Me too."

"You can't be with child because that wouldn't be logical."

"No, it wouldn't." She shook her head, feeling better. "We're going to laugh about this in a few minutes."

Drago smiled. It was forced, his eyes kept this pinched look. "So much."

Ceri got out of the SUV, armed with two of the tests.

"Good luck," Drago called after her.

Ceri took a deep breath and headed for the restrooms.

CHAPTER 18

B ay sat at the bar. He looked down at the tumbler in his hand. At the amber-colored liquid inside. The scent coming off it was pungent. Not normally his drink of choice, but he was feeling nostalgic tonight and had ordered it.

"Nursing that?" the bartender asked, elevating his voice above the noise.

Bay nodded.

"Can I get you something else?" he asked, as he cleared some empty beer bottles away.

"Maybe a water."

The male's lip twitched but he nodded once, ducking down to grab a bottle out of the refrigerator under the bar. He handed it to Bay, who paid. Bay opened the bottle and drank down some of the cool liquid. He scanned the place, almost expecting to see her. It was bustling. People danced, they laughed and talked. They flirted and kissed. As per usual, they'd gone to the place across the road. He'd hung out there for a while. Then he'd told Beck that he was going to the Jolly Roger instead. The male had teased him for a while, but he'd eventually let him go. Here he was.

It seemed he liked to torture himself since he was

standing in exactly the same place she had been standing six months earlier. Bay picked the tumbler back up and took a sip of the whiskey. It burned on the way down. Thing was, Beck was right. He *did* need to move on. It was time. It was past due.

The females sitting right next to him kept whispering to one another. They were arguing over who would get him. Like he didn't have a choice in the matter.

"I saw him first," the blonde said, flicking her hair over her shoulder.

"His eyes met mine when he looked this way earlier," the one with the short, dark hair said, her brown eyes wide.

"I've been single for the longest, so surely that means I get first dibs." The one with the tight curls stepped in-between the other two. Of course, that set off a whole new argument as to why the length of time being single didn't count in who ended up getting him.

He casually glanced their way. They were pretty. All three of them giggled when they caught him looking. They resumed their debate as soon as he turned away.

Another female moved in next to him on the other side. She ordered a couple of drinks. "Thirsty?" he asked, looking at the three bottles that had been placed in front of her. It was a stupid thing to say. He was seriously rusty.

She smiled and nodded. "I'm dancing with my friends, so yeah, very."

He nodded, already chickening out, even though he couldn't scent a male on her.

"And you? Just sitting here...on your own." She glanced at the three females on the other side of him.

"Yep, all alone. I'm from out of town."

He noticed how she looked down at his hand. Humans wore rings to symbolize being mated. They didn't have the same senses as dragons. She was checking to see if he was available.

"Um, can I buy you a drink?" she asked, clearly better at this than he was. She had shoulder-length blonde hair. It had a slight curl. She wore jeans and a tight, red top. Her eyes were wide and a bright blue. She was short and curvy and definitely the type of female he would have been interested in back in the day. Before his run-in with a silver blade. All he could think about though when looking at her was of another female. One with green eyes and dark hair. *Ceri.*

Fuck!

He needed to move on. Ceri wasn't thinking about him. Ceri had moved on. He shook his head. "No," Bay held up the bottle of water, "I'm all set."

Her demeanor changed. Her eyes clouded slightly and her shoulders slumped just a little.

"But I wouldn't mind talking."

Talking. Fuck, but he'd turned into a total pussy. He was a bigger one now that his dick was fully functional than when he'd been half a male. What was wrong with him? He should be happy about it. Should be embracing his new-found virility, but all he could do was mope.

Her eyes lit up. "I'm Carly."

"Bay. Good to meet you." He took her outstretched hand and shook it.

Carly picked up two of the bottles. "I'm going to take these—"

Just then, another female arrived. She smiled at Bay and giggled when her eyes met Carly's. "I'll take those." She winked. Or at least, from where he was sitting it looked like she winked.

Then he realized that he was still sitting while she stood

there. He really was shit at the whole pick-up thing. Bay stood up off the barstool, watching Carly's friend walk back to the dancefloor. "Can I offer you a seat?"

"Thanks." She smiled, climbing up on the stool. "So where are you from?"

He told her their well-rehearsed spiel about where they were from and what they did.

Her eyes lit up. "You're a cage-fighter?" Her gaze moved over his face. "My brother got involved for a couple of months. He fought a couple of times and after being knocked out twice, he retired." She laughed. "I must say you don't look like a fighter since your nose has never been broken and you don't have any scars...that I can see."

"I forgot to mention that I'm a *good* cage fighter. I tend to win."

She nodded. "I'm impressed. I mean, you're a big guy." Her eyes flitted to his chest before moving back up to his face. "How long are you in town for?"

"Just one night." He uncapped his water.

"Pity." She smiled up at him. "It would have been nice to get to know you better."

Bay took a sip of his water. This was the part where he suggested they fuck. One night of hot sex. His dick didn't jump at the plan. In fact, it did nothing.

She took a sip of her drink. Her cheeks began to turn pink. Her eyes moved to her friends and then back to him. "We could get out of here. I have an apartment not ten minutes from here. We could talk."

Talk.

He squeezed the back of his neck. This female was lovely. Truly she was. He wanted to take her up on her offer, but...Bay clenched his teeth. He *should* take her up on her offer. Ceri was done with him. It had just been really great rutting. Nothing more. He needed to stop this obsession he had. It wasn't healthy.

"Or, we could just stay here and hang out?" she quickly added, taking another sip of her drink.

"You know what, Carly?" He put the water down on the bar. "Let's go back to your place."

Her whole face lit up, then she frowned. "Are you sure?"

He nodded. "Yes." He tried to smile, tried to feel something, anything, but failed. By fucking claw, he was going through with this. He was rutting this female and getting over the vampire if it was the last thing he ever did.

"Of course I'm sure. You're gorgeous. Blonde happens to be my favorite." Such a bullshit line.

"Well then," she slid off of the chair, "you're in for a treat, since I'm blonde all over." She winked.

Why were they there?

She was crazy. Worse than crazy. *Nuts!* Then again, she knew, deep down inside, exactly what had driven her to have asked to come all the way out there. Bay was on the Stag Run and she was praying that she would arrive in time to stop him from doing what he had gone there to do. She should go back and wait until morning, but instead, she had insisted that time was of the essence – which it was – but it could have waited until the next day. A few hours wouldn't have mattered, and yet she'd insisted.

Hopefully, she wasn't too late.

They arrived at the bar. "This is it," Reef said. He was one of the Water dragons who had been assigned to help them.

"Beach Bums," Drago read the sign that hung above the door. "How original." It was a different place to the one she had met Bay in. The Jolly Roger was just across the street. She looked that way, feeling her heart squeeze. Butterflies took flight in her stomach, big ones. Hyperactive ones. She felt a moment of nausea.

Drago sensed her hesitation, he put an arm around her and squeezed once before letting go. "Ready?"

No!

She nodded. "Thanks for coming. I know you were busy with—"

"Of course I came along. Don't mention it. You needed the support and here I am. I hope we're…on time."

She nodded once. It was already getting late. It was probably too late. Bay was a catch. The humans would be all over him.

"Let's go inside. We might be lucky enough to still find him here," Wade said. He was another of the Water dragons helping them.

"He might have already left," Reef voiced what they were all thinking. "We could still catch up with him at the hotel, although—" The male stopped talking, must have caught the horrified look on her face.

If Bay was already back at the hotel, there was a good chance he wasn't going to be there alone, and neither would he be sleeping. More butterflies and more nausea hit her.

"Maybe we shouldn't be here." No doubt about it. Bay had decided to attend the Stag Run for one reason and one reason only. He was there to rut a human female. Heck, he might be there to rut a couple. She'd pined for him all of these months and here he was, hitting the town, at the first chance he could get. According to Torrent, they went on a Run every six months and this was his weekend. It had been six months, almost to the day, since they had first met.

"We're here already. Might as well go in and take a look," Drago said. He was her voice of reason.

"You're right." She nodded.

Drago took her hand and they walked into the still bustling bar. Reef walked ahead of them and Wade followed behind.

Reef scanned the room, quickly deciding which direction to take. Ceri tried to give the air a sniff in the hope of picking up his scent, but there were too many feuding smells. Aside from lots of different people, many of the females wore perfume. There was also a strong scent of greasy food.

They followed Reef, who made a beeline for a large male. The male's eyes narrowed as they landed on Reef. He removed his arm from around a female and stepped forward. "Is everything okay?"

"We're looking for Bay," Reef said.

His eyes narrowed further, they moved over Reef's shoulder before landing on her and then Drago. He sniffed the air. "Vampires. What are they doing here? What's going on?"

"That's a need-to-know." Reef shook his head. "I'm not at liberty to say. We're here on Torrent's orders."

"Is Bay in trouble?"

"Um…not exactly," Reef said.

"What does that mean?" the male asked. "Just tell me what the hell's going on."

"Where is Bay? It's important that we find him. Please, Beck."

Beck held the male's gaze for a long while before

looking at Ceri. "Are you her?"

She nodded once.

"For whatever reason," Beck looked back at Reef, "he wanted to go to the bar across the road. I can't remember what he said it was called."

Her heart beat faster. *Their bar.* He wanted to go to their bar. Did that mean he was thinking about her?

Reef finished whatever it was he was saying to Beck and then motioned for them to head out. Her feet felt somewhat lighter as they crossed the road. It didn't last though. The butterflies took flight as they made it to the door. It was big and blue. Was he still there? Had he left? If so, was he alone?

"Let's go," Drago said to Reef, who nodded. They filed into the busy bar. It was even more packed than the one across the road had been.

"Maybe we should rather wait until morning." His smile was tight.

Ceri kept looking, she spotted him at the bar. Standing in the same spot they had stood in six months earlier. Only, instead of her, there was a cute human female. She was ultra-curvy with a sweet smile.

Bay wore black jeans and a white t-shirt. It fit him like a second skin, showcasing muscle and brawn. His skin had a bronze glow. His eyes were bright and just as gorgeous as she remembered.

The human nodded at something Bay was saying. Ceri had to concentrate to hear what she was saying. "I'm impressed. I mean, you're a big guy." Her eyes flitted to his chest before moving back up to his face. The female was flirting with him. Of course she was. Who wouldn't? She hadn't been able to help herself all those months ago. "How long are you in town for?"

"Just one night." He picked up his water.

"Pity." The female smiled at him, looking up at him from under her lashes. More flirting. "It would have been nice to get to know you better."

"Let's go and—" Reef began.

Ceri held up a hand to keep him quiet. "Give me a minute."

This was going to go one of two ways. She could see Bay weighing things up. Mulling them over. The female looked unsure. Not of Bay, but of the situation. She was afraid of being rejected.

Ceri needed to put a stop to this but she couldn't, she needed to see how this played out. She had not been able to move on. The thought was abhorrent. If Bay had real feelings for her, he wouldn't be able to either. She needed to see this for herself.

"We should—" Drago began.

"Please be quiet," she urged.

"We could get out of here," she heard the human say, twirling a piece of her hair around a finger. "I have an apartment not ten minutes from here. We could talk."

The funny thing was that had been her line six months ago. Maybe not exactly but similar. Her heart was pounding. She sucked in a deep breath.

Bay squeezed the back of his neck, he looked tired. That and stressed. For a couple of seconds there she was sure he would turn the female down flat.

The human seemed to think that too because she said, "Or, we could just stay here and hang out?"

"You know what, Carly?" Bay put the water down on the bar, seeming to make up his mind. Ceri didn't have a good feeling about where this was going. "Let's go back to your place." He nodded once, looking resolute.

The female's whole face lit up. "Are you sure?" she gushed.

He nodded. "Yes," Bay smiled, "of course I'm sure. You're gorgeous. Blonde happens to be my favorite."

Talk about a dagger to the heart.

"Well then," she slid off the chair, a seductive look in her eyes, "you're in for a treat, since I'm blonde all over." The human winked.

The dagger was silver-tipped. At least that's what it felt like, especially when Bay grinned.

"You should go over there," Drago interjected, clutching her elbow, trying to lead.

"No!" Ceri shook her head, suddenly feeling claustrophobic. She shoved her way to the door and practically ran outside. All three males followed her.

Ceri gulped lungfuls of air.

"What's wrong?" Drago asked. "He's here and he hasn't technically done anything yet. You can still stop him."

"I don't want to," Ceri said, shaking her head.

"You said you have feelings for him. You finally admitted it!" Drago practically yelled. "He's in there."

"About to leave with another female."

Oh shit! Bay was about to leave. He'd find them there. She didn't want that. Didn't want to ruin his night. Ceri started towards the SUV.

"Where are you going?" Drago asked.

"We're leaving," she announced. "I'll talk with him in the morning and then we're going home." She felt her lip quiver but held back the tears threatening to fall.

"You can still fix this," Drago tried one last time as they climbed into the vehicle.

"There is nothing to fix." She shook her head, feeling

miserable. "Let's just please leave. Please," she added the last when no one did anything.

Reef nodded. He started the vehicle and they pulled away. The tears began to fall. "I'm sorry," Drago said, taking her hand. "I wish things could be different."

CHAPTER 19

The next morning…

B ay felt exhausted. It had been one long-ass night. He yawned as he left his room.

Delta was just leaving his room as well. The male grinned when he spotted Bay approaching. "Good morning." He sounded upbeat and chipper, even though his eyes were bloodshot.

"Morning." Bay smiled.

"I wish we could stay another night." Delta scratched his head. "One night is nowhere near enough."

"We have to get back to work," Bay muttered.

Delta nodded. "Yeah, I guess we do. Do you have any idea when the next Hunt is planned? I really want another shot at trying to catch a female."

Bay shook his head. "They've been canceled until further notice."

They heard someone approach. Bay looked in that direction. It was Beck. The male was frowning, which was strange. In fact, he didn't look happy at all. "Did she find you?" he asked as his eyes narrowed on Bay. "Is everything okay?"

"Did who find me?" Bay shook his head. "Was

someone looking for me?"

"Your vampire came to Beach Bums last night looking for you." He paused. "By the look on your face, I can tell you have no idea what I'm talking about. You obviously didn't see her."

"Ceri?" Bay frowned. "She was here?"

"Yep." Beck nodded. "It looked serious. Both Reef and Wade were with her, along with a vampire male. Torrent knows about it. The vampires were sent here on his orders. I sent them across the road to where you said you were going. I wonder what happened to them."

His heart beat faster. *Ceri. There.* Ceri was there, or at least she had been. She was looking for him with an entourage of dragons from his tribe. *Why?* "I wasn't there long. I left within a half hour or so, it could be that they missed me." He scrubbed a hand over his face. Adrenaline pumped. "I can't believe she was here." He paced towards the parking lot, then stopped and turned back. "I know we're supposed to be leaving now but I have to go back to the Jolly Roger."

Beck widened his eyes for a few seconds. "To do what? She won't be there. It's a Sunday morning. The bars and clubs will all be closed."

"I have to go and look. Maybe she's at the hotel she stayed in last time." He pushed a hand through his hair, trying to come up with a plan. "I can't just leave if she's here."

"You're talking crazy." Beck pointed to the line of SUVs, to all the males waiting to leave. "I told you she was with males from our tribe, chances are good that she's back at the lair, or someone there will at least be able to fill you in on why she was here in the first place. Wade and Reef looked serious, they all did. I'm sure there is a valid explanation."

"I can't believe I missed her." Bay shook his head. His instincts told him to look for her. To keep looking until he found her, but Beck was right, his approach was the rational one. Bay sucked in a deep breath, trying to clear his head, trying to get his heartrate under control. He finally nodded once, breathing out through his nose.

They all piled into the SUVs and made the forty-minute trip into the mountains. The dragons had bought a large property there. Acres upon acres of land. They had built garages for their fleet of vehicles. There was also a large cabin they used to change and shower. A caretaker took care of the place, staying on the property. The caretaker was a dragon. From time to time a new dragon would be appointed the assignment.

Bay pushed the remote and watched the garage door slowly open. He parked next to another vehicle that had arrived just ahead of them. He and three males exited the vehicle. Beck glanced at his watch. "We're running late," he announced. "There's no time for lunch. We need to leave in five?" He raised his brows.

Bay nodded, he was thankful the male had stepped in to take the leadership role. He was still feeling shell-shocked.

They headed for the house. One of the Earth dragons stood just outside the front door on the porch. He had been assigned to live in the house for a period. The duty usually lasted a couple of weeks at a time as caretaker of the property. Bay couldn't remember this male's name. He lifted his hand in greeting.

Beck was walking just ahead of him, the rest of the males trailed behind. They would undress at the cabin, leaving all of their clothing for the Earth dragon to launder. Once a quick check of the perimeter was made, they'd leave for home. Bay suddenly felt a sense of urgency. Maybe Ceri was back at the lair. He had to get there and find out. He needed to know what the hell was going on. Worry ate at him.

He moved in ahead of Beck, climbing the stairs that led to the porch, two at a time. Just then, the door opened and a dark-haired male walked out. The male's eyes were narrowed and focused on him. Three strides later and the male had closed the space between them.

Vampire.

Bay caught his scent—*Bam!* The male hit him. The punch landed square on his jaw. Hard too. Bay staggered back a step but kept his footing. "Wait, I—" he tried.

Bam!

The male hit him again. This time in the mouth. Bay tasted blood. *Who the fuck was this asshole?* Bay growled, blocking the next punch. He pulled back, intent on giving the fucker a taste of his own damned medicine but someone grabbed his arm. The Earth dragon gripped the vampire under his armpits, holding him back as well.

Bay snarled.

The vampire snarled right back, fangs bared. "You fucking bastard!" the male growled. "How could you?"

Did he know this male? "Who the fuck are you?" Bay growled back at the still struggling vampire.

Then the male's expression changed. He stopped trying to break free. His nostrils flared and a look of shock and puzzlement caused his brow to crease. "You don't scent of human," he mumbled. "Why don't you scent of female?"

"Stop this!" a female yelled. "No more, Drago."

Bay pulled in a deep breath. It was his turned to be

shocked. He lifted his eyes and there she was. Ceri. She was there standing just a few feet away from him. Wearing a light blue summer dress and a light knit jersey, she looked even more beautiful than he remembered. "Ceri? What's going on?" Then his own senses kicked in. This was the male he had often scented on her. Her friend? Maybe he was more? He snarled at the male. "Who are you, asshole?"

Beck grabbed Bay from behind, holding onto him. "Calm down!" he yelled, right next to his ear.

"I'm sorry," Drago addressed Ceri. "I lost it when I saw this jerk. After watching how his actions made you…" He stopped talking and glared at Bay.

"What actions? What happened?" Bay asked. "Would somebody mind telling me what the hell is going on?" He looked Ceri in the eye and then at Reef who was standing behind her in the doorway.

"We need to talk," Ceri said, her expression was grave.

"Has everyone calmed the fuck down?" Beck asked.

"Yes," Bay growled, sounding anything but calm. It couldn't be helped. Something was up. Something major. Worry churned in his gut.

"Do you plan on throwing any more punches, vampire?" Beck asked.

Drago grit his teeth. "Don't hurt her." He pointed a finger at Bay. "Do you hear me?"

"It's okay, Drago, I've got this." Ceri gripped the male's bicep and squeezed.

A growl was torn from Bay at the sight of Ceri touching the male.

The Earth dragon let the vampire go, the male turned to Ceri. "Call if you need me."

"I will." Ceri nodded.

"I mean it." The male took her hand and Bay had to work hard not to growl again. Not to launch himself at the male and tear his head clean off. He grit his teeth instead. It was an unfair fight. The vampire would be dead in seconds.

"I mean it, dragon." Drago looked his way. "Don't you dare—" He let Ceri's hand go.

Bay snarled, feeling his teeth lengthen, feeling his scales rub.

"Stop!" Ceri moved to stand between them. "Both of you." She put a hand on his chest. Her touch felt good. All too soon she was drawing back.

Bay suddenly realized where he was. He glanced behind him, at the males who had attended the Stag Run. All of them watched with keen interest. "Beck." He locked eyes with the male. "Take over."

Beck nodded. "Don't worry, I will see the males home," his second in command announced. "You stay and…deal with this. I'll see you at the lair."

Bay nodded once. "Thank you."

He turned to Ceri. "I think we should go for a walk." The cabin was big but not nearly big enough. It would take the males at least fifteen minutes to prepare for the trip home. He didn't want any of them hearing what was said. Not the males, not the Earth dragon and certainly not that asshole, Drago. This was between him and Ceri. Bay was racking his brain, but he couldn't think of a single thing she would have to say to him. She wasn't there for sex, or because she was in love with him. That much was clear. *Why then?*

They walked in silence for a few minutes, taking a path that led into the forest. It reminded him of the last time they had been together.

He couldn't scent that male on her. Not like before. He wondered why. Her scent had changed. Maybe she was drinking from someone else. *Who?* He felt his hackles rise even though he couldn't scent that she had rutted. Not recently, at any rate. It calmed him somewhat.

"What's going on?" he finally blurted, unable to hold back any longer. "Why was that male so upset with me?"

"I'm sorry about Drago. He was upset because I was upset." She rubbed her lips together and pulled in a deep breath.

"Why were you upset? It wasn't anything I did, was it?" He shook his head, frowning.

"I have no right to be upset or angry, and Drago had no right to hit you." A strange expression crossed her face. He thought he saw her hands shake right before she clasped them together.

"You look nervous. Why are you nervous? You said you were upset...why?" This wasn't making any sense.

"I'm upset because apparently blonde humans are sometimes blonde all over, not just on their heads." Her eyes blazed for a moment in...anger. Then it was gone.

"Oh." Realization hit. He swallowed hard. "You were there last night."

She nodded.

"You saw—"

"I saw enough," she pushed out. "That's not why I'm here though. Your...sex life has nothing to do with me. I shouldn't have said that."

"I didn't rut that female," he countered. "If you had stayed that little bit longer you would have seen me—"

"It doesn't matter." Her voice was flat.

"It clearly does because you were upset. You are upset about it now even though you're pretending not to be."

"I'm not upset about that." She pressed her lips together "I'm upset about something else."

"The reason for you being here?"

She nodded. "We're idiots!" She put up a hand to silence him. "I'm the bigger idiot of the two of us. It just never occurred to me." She looked down at the ground. "Never in my wildest dreams."

"What's going on, Ceri? Why are we idiots? Why are you here?" It definitely had nothing to do with anything he hoped it would be. She'd made that clear…yet again.

"You need to know that you don't owe me anything. I am perfectly capable and perfectly…"

He watched feeling concern as a tear slid down her cheek. "Okay, you need to talk to me, Ceri. You need to tell me what's going on. I'm getting worried here. Enough riddles and talking around things. You need to—"

"I'm pregnant and it's yours."

The air left his lungs. His legs suddenly felt weak. Bay sat down, right there on the ground with a thump. His head spun. His mind raced. His mouth suddenly dried right up. He put his head in his hands, trying to control his breathing. Trying to control the racing of his heart.

Oh crap! Crap!

His shoulders rose and fell quickly. Bay was upset. Of course he was. For years he'd thought he was incapable of having kids of his own and now—She could see that it was too much for him. They hardly knew one another. A vampire was having his baby. A bloodsucker. Someone he hardly knew.

Oh god! A baby.

Her stomach did that clenching thing again. Ceri pulled

herself together. She could do this. *She could!* "Look, I can see how upset you are. I understand. I had a similar reaction when I found out yesterday."

His head was still in his hands.

"You need to know that I can handle this." Could she though? *Yes!* Her stomach clenched harder and she tasted bile. "I thought that you should know. It—"

Bay closed the distance between them, still on the ground. He nuzzled his face into her belly. He put his arms around her. "That scent. That's what I could smell. You are with child. My child." He looked up at her, his eyes were glistening just a little bit, like he wanted to cry but was holding himself back.

"You're excited about this? Happy?" She bit down on her lip. She hoped that he would be open to being involved in this whole thing. Ceri had never expected this level of excitement though.

"Yes!" He nodded, climbing to his feet. "I'm thrilled. How are you feeling? Are you—"

"I'm fine," she assured him. "Okay, so you're happy." It was a good thing. She gathered her thoughts. "I think I must have become pregnant the last time we were together. When you were cured, I guess I was cured as well. It never occurred to me that taking each other's blood would cure me too. Stupid though, if you think about it. Then again, the whole thing was a long shot. Curing you, that is. I don't think I really expected it to work."

"Neither did I. It came as a shock."

She clasped and unclasped her hands before folding her arms to stop herself from fidgeting. "That makes me three months along. Although I'm not sure what that means."

Bay grinned, his smile was beautiful, it lit up his whole

face. His eyes danced. "It means we're three months away from becoming parents."

"Most likely, yes." She licked her lips. "So far, even with cross-matings, the young tend to take the characteristics of the father. For the most part, at least. You need to know—"

"You're having my whelp." Wonder-filled his voice. "I'm going to be a father. I can't believe it."

She nodded, feeling her mouth turn up at the corners, his excitement catching. "Hopefully, if all goes well." There was a flipside to this coin.

His eyes clouded in an instant. "What do you mean if all goes well?"

"I had the operation to remove my womb because my pelvis is too narrow. It was deemed too risky to ever attempt bringing a baby into this world. I have watched females die trying." A lump formed in her throat, the words catching.

"Are you at risk?" His voice had turned gravelly. Scales appeared on his chest.

"I met with your healers today."

Bay's jaw tightened. His eyes hardened. He looked pissed. "What did they say?" His voice was gruff. "Are you in any danger?"

She was shocked by his reaction. He was probably worried about the baby. "A dragon female is pregnant for six months and a vampire female for twelve, we are hopeful this pregnancy will be shorter than a vampire one. Hoping the baby will be smaller than—"

"A dragon whelp *is* small. Much smaller than human children, I am told. Surely—"

"Vampire young are the largest of all the young. A terrible design for sure, since we have the narrowest hips."

She clutched her sides. "We have no way of knowing how this pregnancy will progress." She shook her head. "Charlotte, a vampire female, had a similar thing happen to her. Her pelvis is also too small to have had a vampire child. She mated an elf and her womb began functioning again, same as mine did. Again," she shook her head, "I feel like an idiot for not thinking of it. It just never crossed my mind. Not once!" She swallowed. "Anyway, she birthed a healthy elven child. A female. Elves only carry for four months though. The birth was not easy, but it was possible. And then Stephany – another female with narrow hips – birthed twins for the wolf alpha. She carried for three months. It was a smooth birth. No complications. This," she pointed between them, "combination has never been tested. Even six months might end up being too long."

"A Fire dragon female had the whelp of a vampire male." He sounded animated. "It was a success. The whelp is more vampire than dragon. They are happily mated. I heard the other day that Ruby is with child again."

"It's all very encouraging. Like I said, I'm hopeful." She cleared her throat, putting a hand on her belly. A slight curve. She'd felt more movement. Was already in love with this child. She prayed for what felt like the hundredth time since finding out that she was pregnant. Prayed for a healthy baby, most especially a normal birth.

"It's going to work out." He touched the side of her arm, quickly pulling back.

Ceri nodded, forcing a smile. "I will stay in touch with you and keep you informed. We should probably exchange contact information." She giggled. It came out sounding nervous as hell and maybe a little hysterical. "We have no idea—"

"No." He shook his head, his eyes narrowing onto hers.

"What do you mean, no? I thought you were happy. That you would want to know what was happening."

"I want more than to stay in touch. I'm staying with you, Ceri. I'm the father."

"That won't work." She shook her head.

"It's going to have to work. Either I'm going to move in with you or you're moving in with me. You can choose which you would prefer." He folded his arms.

"Hold up." She took a step back. "No way! We hardly know one another, we—"

"Best we get started then. We have a couple of months to get to know each other. You are the mother of my child. We need to make this work."

Her head spun. She took another step back. "No. Forget it! There is no 'us.'"

"I'm not forgetting anything and there soon will be an 'us,' if I have anything to say about it." His eyes seemed lighter.

"You almost rutted another female last night." Okay, that came out sounding jealous. "Not that I'm judging you, because I'm not. You were free...*are* free to do whatever you want. I didn't and certainly still don't have any hold on you."

"You *do* have a hold on me, a huge hold, you're carrying my whelp," he growled.

"That doesn't mean anything!" she yelled.

"It means everything!" he yelled back.

"You know what I mean." More softly delivered.

He nodded. "I know exactly what you mean, and it's bullshit."

"We don't love one another. I do not plan on holding you in a loveless mating because of this child. We can still be good parents to him or her."

His chest heaved. His eyes had lost their sparkle. "Fine, we can live together as friends then. See where it goes."

It hurt so badly to hear him concede – essentially that's what he had done – to not having feelings for her. "How is that going to work?" Her voice was shrill. *Why was he being pigheaded about this?* "And I would just wave goodbye every six months while you go off on your Stag Run. Then one day you'll bring someone home and you'll mate her. We'll all live together as one big happy messed up family? What if I want to bring someone home?"

He snarled like he was jealous at the thought. His eyes were definitely lighter, glowing a little under the deep shade of the forest. He walked a few steps in the opposite direction before turning back. Bay pulled in a deep breath. "We'll figure it out. I won't be separated from my child. I'm going to assume you won't be fucking around while with child. I can promise the same. I need to keep an eye on you, to make sure nothing happens and that you are both safe. We can talk again once our child is born."

Ceri was happy he cared so much about the baby. It hurt that it seemed like that's all he cared about. "Don't hold yourself back on my account."

He made a noise of frustration. "It wouldn't be on your account."

"On the baby's and my account then." *Shit!* This wasn't going as planned. That was an awful thing to say. "Please forget I said that. I didn't mean it. Let's give this some thought."

"I don't need to think about it. I'm taking a leave of absence. I'll move in with you."

Her heart raced. She loved the idea of this. Loved it way too much. It scared her as well. He was doing this for their child. Only for the baby. They may never have seen each other again if it hadn't been for this pregnancy. "I don't have a spare bedroom."

"You have a couch and I'm taking it. We'll move to my lair when we are closer to the birth."

"Don't I have a say in any of this?" She knew she was being difficult. This was such a mess.

He took her hand in his. It was big and warm and comforting. "Of course you do. I want you happy and comfortable. Being in your own space will afford you that. Then I want you safe. Both of you." He glanced down at her belly. "You are carrying a dragon whelp. We should be here for the birth. We have human doctors and dragon healers. Again, it is something we can discuss."

For a few moments, she felt like she was struggling to breathe. Not so long ago she thought that she could never have a baby. Now she was a couple of months away from giving birth. There were no guarantees on how any of this would turn out. Could she live with a male she had feelings for? The father of her baby. Could she live with Bay knowing he more than likely would never return her feelings? While, at the same time, there was a good chance her feelings would deepen.

"You are not alone. We will do this together." He squeezed her hand. Why then did she feel loneliness so acute it hurt? She swallowed back tears and nodded. "Does that mean you agree?" His beautiful eyes lit up.

"Yes." The word sounded choked. "It's the hormones." She shook her head. At least she still had Drago.

CHAPTER 20

His fist slammed against the desk, rattling the wood. Papers scattered. "I asked you not to fuck it up and you did," Torrent raged. "You fucked it up royally," he snarled. "You rutted a vampire. What the fuck were you thinking? How was it even possible? We all thought you…you were…"

"Blood," Bay muttered. "That's how."

"What?" Torrent frowned.

"I won't get into the details, but—"

Torrent seemed to realize what he was referring to and put up a hand. "Don't tell me. You were with a vampire. I can guess. I don't want to know the details."

Not that he planned on divulging any. It was between him and Ceri. "I'm happy about this." Bay couldn't help but smile. "Thrilled at the prospect of being a father."

"Once she cured you, you could have moved on and had a nice human. Like my Candy."

The thought left him cold. "I don't want a human. I want to try to make things work with the vampire." It was a long shot, but one he was going to take.

"It doesn't sound like she wants the same. Brant said she was very apprehensive about you living with her."

"I want to be there for the child. I need to ensure this

pregnancy runs smoothly." If nothing else, this was his top priority. "I will insist on being there for the birth."

Torrent made a face. "You can't be serious."

"I have done some research and it is not frowned upon for vampire males to attend the births of their young."

"You are a dragon!" Torrent boomed.

"This is a high-risk pregnancy. Many things can go wrong. I will be there! I will insist!"

"Let's see what the vampire has to say about it. I know our healers will be against it."

"Does this mean that you will let me go and live with her?" Bay had already decided he was leaving whether Torrent granted him permission or not. His place was at Ceri's side. He only hoped he could convince her to mate him before the baby arrived. He wanted a family. He wanted Ceri.

"For the record, I think you are making a mistake. You do not have to live with her. You can still be a good father," Torrent echoed what Ceri had said.

Thing was, Bay didn't care what Torrent thought. This was his decision and his decision alone. He had already made up his mind. Bay couldn't say any of that, so he let his silence speak.

"I can see that you have made up your mind?"

Bay nodded. "Yes, I have."

"Do I have a choice but to let you go?" Torrent's eyes blazed.

Bay looked down at the floor for a moment before meeting his king's gaze. "My place is with my unborn child."

Torrent nodded. "As your king, I am angered by this. As a male who is a father, I understand. I am giving you permission to leave. I am putting Beck in your place…temporarily. Flood will take second."

"They are bound to clash." *Shit!* It was never going to work. Unfortunately, it couldn't be his problem, not right then. Not with so much at stake.

"They need to sort out their shit. You must know though, that if you leave, you will forfeit your leadership role. I will not reinstate you." Torrent shook his head. "I am not punishing you, because I didn't technically forbid you from rutting. I didn't think I had to," he muttered the last.

In the end, it was almost a relief to hear. Bay was not a male to back down from a challenge. Nor was he a quitter, but he did not enjoy his role as leader. Beck or Flood were far better suited. It was the main reason the two of them butted heads as much as they did. They were very different in some ways but exactly the same in others. "I understand."

"You are leaving anyway."

"I must." Bay nodded.

Five days later…

There was a knock on the door and she almost jumped out of her skin. This was it. She squeezed her eyes shut, willing her heart to stop going nuts.

"Coming." She walked to the door and opened it.

Bay smiled as soon as their eyes met. *Why did he have to be so darned gorgeous?* Tall, dark and delicious. His scent enveloped her. Even though she didn't drink much blood anymore, her fangs sharpened anyway. She was thirsty again for the first time in weeks. Not like before, but still—

She realized she was gaping. Who could blame her? He wore a pair of those cotton pants. They were white. *Holy cow! White!* His skin was golden against the fabric, his abs were…well, they were perfect. He'd been working out even more since she had last had sex with him, that much was clear. Why was she thinking about sex? It had to stop immediately.

His smiled turned to a grin. "Can I come in?" He glanced over her shoulder and into her apartment for a few seconds.

She blinked. "Sorry! This is a bit weird."

"I guess it is. Look, we'll get to know each other and then it won't be so…" He let the sentence die.

Stilted. Awkward. Ceri knew he didn't say those things out loud, but it was what he was thinking. There was also an underlying tension between them. Ceri was still attracted to him. She wondered if he felt the same.

She held his gaze a moment longer and then nodded once, reminding herself why Bay was really there. For a moment, just a few seconds, she'd felt possibilities. Not very intelligent of her. Just the other day Bay had attended the Stag Run. He had almost rutted another female. She wasn't sure why he had changed his mind. Make no mistake, it was he who had rejected the human and not the other way around. Sure, Ceri had felt relief when she hadn't been able to scent the other female on him, but she couldn't shake the fact that he had been there in the first place. It was a weekend designed for mindless rutting. One he had felt the need to attend.

More importantly, he was there for the baby. *That was all!* He had made it clear that he was going to try to win her. It would be for all the wrong reasons though and she had to keep reminding herself of that. "Is this my bed?"

He pointed at the couch.

She'd put a pillow, a sheet and blanket in a neat pile on the armrest.

Ceri nodded. "Brant is organizing us bigger accommodation. I would prefer two units next to one another—"

His jaw tightened. "No, we need to get properly acquainted. It would be better if we were under the same roof."

"Okay, well then, this is it for now, I'm afraid. You can use that dresser," she pointed at the piece of furniture in the far corner, "for your things. Can I show you around?"

"Sure." He shrugged, pulling a bag from his shoulder and placing it on the floor next to the sofa.

"Through here," she opened the door, "is the kitchen. I'm afraid it's probably smaller than you are used to. I saw the apartments in your lair and—"

"I don't mind."

"It's comfortable but certainly not as lavish as what you're accustomed to."

"Such things are really not important to me." Bay shook his head.

"I place a weekly order for groceries. Let me know what you like and I'll order it for you. We have two restaurants on the property as well. One in the castle. The other one— you already know—it's in the hotel."

"Perfect. Sounds good." He smiled, following her back into the lounge area. There was a small four-seater dining room table to the one side.

"This is the guest bathroom." She opened the door. "It's literally just a toilet and a sink. We'll have to share my en-suite bathroom, which has both a bath and a shower." They walked into her bedroom. She pointed at the closed door on the far side.

"We'll manage." Bay shrugged like it was no big deal.

She felt the now familiar thump, thump inside her tummy. Her son or daughter making themselves known. Ceri felt her heart squeeze. She put a hand on her belly.

"What is it?" Bay frowned. "Is everything okay."

"The baby is kicking." She smiled.

His eyes lit up, reminding her of a small child. "Please can I…" He was looking at her belly.

She was shocked at how much it had grown in such a short time. There was a definite curve. So much so, that she was beginning to look pregnant. Ceri nodded. "Here." She took his hand and placed it on the spot where the little one had just kicked.

Thump.

"There," she said. "Did you feel it?"

Bay frowned. "I don't think so."

"They're still very soft."

Thump. Thump. A bit harder that time. "Did you…?" She could see he was frowning even deeper than before. "Wait." She sat down on the bed and lifted her top, pulling down her tights a little. Then she took his hand and placed it directly on her skin. His eyes were narrowed in deep concentration.

Thump.

Bay's eyes widened.

Thump.

He sucked in a breath. "I can feel him. I feel the kicks!" he choked out. His eyes stayed wide, she could see he was barely breathing.

Thump. Thump.

Bay choked out a laugh. "That's amazing! He's kicking."

"Or she." Ceri found that she was smiling too.

"Or she, although dragon females are rare, one is hardly ever born. Never from a human female."

"I am a vampire," Ceri said. Then she realized that his hand was still firmly on her stomach with her hand pressing over his. His thigh was also up against hers. It suddenly felt close and intimate. Her mouth felt a bit dry. Other parts of her felt other things. Things they shouldn't be feeling. Her nipples tightened. There was an achy feeling between her legs.

It was those blasted hormones. She was extra horny since becoming pregnant. Ceri jumped up, fixing her clothing.

Bay stood up as well. "I'll just get unpacked then."

CHAPTER 21

Two days later…

Something woke her. She felt instantly wide awake. Her curtains were a grey shade, telling her that the sun had started rising but that it was still early. There it was again, that sound she'd heard earlier. She lifted her head.

"Shit, I'm sorry." Bay held up a hand, looking sheepish. "I didn't mean to wake you."

Ceri decided right then that she hated him. Bay had insisted on living with her so that he could drive her batshit crazy. His hair was wet. Droplets ran down his chest. The towel was fluffy and white. It was fastened around his hips. Low on his hips. Low enough that she could see every single one of his abs in all of their wet glory.

"Um," she cleared her throat, "that's okay."

"I'm meeting Brant," Bay mumbled. "Thought it best if I showered before meeting with one of the kings. I tried to be quiet, I swear I did. You go back to sleep." He took another step.

"That's okay. It's almost time for me to get up anyways. Why the meeting?" she asked, sitting up.

His gaze dropped to her boobs, lingering there before

returning to her eyes. Ceri wore a light purple sleeping shirt. The garment had become tight around her breasts and snug around her belly. "Ah…" He lifted his gaze, looking like he couldn't remember what it was he wanted to say. Two small frown lines appeared between his eyes.

"The meeting." She smiled, raising her brows. It was good to know that it wasn't just her who was still affected by this attraction. Bay looked like he was still feeling it, even though her body was changing. They had never struggled in the chemistry department.

"Oh, yeah, um, I'm hoping he'll allow me to work while I'm here. I want to be close to you, but I can't sit around all day doing nothing."

"You can come and help me at the clinic," she blurted. "I could use an extra pair of hands."

Bay laughed. "I'm not so sure about that. I think there might be an opening on the Elite team. I'm probably better suited as a warrior than a healer."

"You won't get a spot on the Elite team. No offense – those types of positions are hard-won."

He flexed his muscles. "Good thing I'm up for the challenge."

"Good luck then!"

"What do you have planned today?" He ran a hand through his still dripping hair, trying to finger-comb it.

"Oh, I need to get to work. I have a ton of appointments today, but first, breakfast." She rolled her eyes. "I don't know how you do it. Vampires drink every couple of days. We do eat solid food, but we certainly don't need three square meals, and then don't forget the snacks in-between. It's so time-consuming."

"Oh, that's interesting." He folded his arms and took a step towards her bed. "So you don't drink blood anymore?"

"I do but very little and not very often. I think my requirements have changed because I'm pregnant with a dragon shifter baby. Human females crave blood when they are pregnant by vampires."

Bay made a sound of agreement and took another step, putting him right at the foot of her bed. His eyes were so blue. His shoulders broad. His—*Enough, Ceri!*

"It is similar when human females are pregnant with dragon whelps." He thankfully hadn't noticed her…discomfort. "They crave more meat and prefer it to be more on the rare side. They go off milk…dairy products in general."

"That explains my cravings for steak. I can't get enough of it. That and ham sandwiches, with plenty of ham."

He gave her a half-smile. "How are you feeling otherwise?"

"I'm good."

He scrutinized her. "Do you mean that?"

"No, I do. I'm great. My energy levels are back up. I had a few days of nausea a while back, but I put that to…" *Missing you. Your blood. You.* She couldn't say any of that. "I wasn't sure what was going on, but it was over before I thought anything of it."

"What about how you're feeling, on the inside?"

"My feelings?" Was he still talking about the baby? She assumed he was. "I'm still scared…for the little one," she put a hand on her belly, "and for myself as well. I know how badly things can go. I've seen the worst-case scenario firsthand."

"I know, and I wish that wasn't the case. You won't be pregnant nearly as long as a vampire female normally would be. It's going to work out. We have to believe that."

"We don't know anything, at this stage, but I think you are right. Stressing about it isn't going to solve anything." Her mouth felt dry just thinking about it. Her stomach felt like a rock had lodged itself inside her.

"Okay, well, I'd better get dressed." He looked down at himself. "I'm leaving in ten minutes. Have a good day."

"Thank you." She smiled. "Good luck with your meeting. I must warn you, Brant comes across like an asshole if you don't know him. He was very upset about this pregnancy. He shouted and broke a table, but then he got over himself. Now he's really worried about me."

"My kings weren't too thrilled either."

"He will probably act like a complete jerk initially. Don't take it personally. Don't let that get to you, he's actually quite a nice male deep down. He just doesn't often show that side of himself."

"Yep, my king is the same. They feel they need to come across as being in charge and in control. They act like they don't have emotions."

"Except for maybe anger."

He grinned. "Yep! Like I said, I was in big shit for," he widened his eyes, "for all of this."

"Oh…sorry."

"It's not your fault. It takes two to…make a baby." He got this strange look, but it was gone before she could place it. "See you later."

She nodded. "Yep."

He paused and turned back just before he got to the door. Bay glanced back at her. "I'll make dinner tonight. I can barbecue a mean steak."

"That would be great." *It's not a date. It doesn't mean anything, he's just being nice.*

Ceri pulled in a breath. "It really would be lovely,

thanks." Why was she being so polite? This was so awkward.

Bay left, closing her bedroom door behind him. She fell back onto the pillows. Ceri was thrilled about this pregnancy. The life growing inside her was truly a miracle. Hopefully the birth would be smooth and without incident. *Not thinking about that!* The situation with Bay was difficult though, to say the least. The next few months were going to feel long and drawn-out.

CHAPTER 22

Five days later...

"So, where is he?" Drago asked, looking around her apartment.

"He who?" Ceri answered even though she knew exactly who Drago was talking about.

Drago looked at her like she'd lost her mind. "You know who! Where's the father of your unborn child? The male you're living with?"

"Oh, Bay?"

"Yes, the dragon. Of course the dragon. Who else?" Drago had referred to Bay as *the dragon* ever since the fight.

"He's at training."

Drago snorted. "I hear he's hoping to make it onto the Elite team. What bullshit! He's not one of us."

"Don't start!"

"Don't start what?" His face turned all innocent. *Yeah, right!*

"Like you pointed out not one minute ago, he's the father of this baby. It shouldn't matter what species he is. I would prefer it if you didn't bad-mouth him."

"I guess it irritates me that you spent months pining for the guy – don't try to deny it, I now know it for what it was. The not eating or sleeping, the whole 'working yourself to a standstill' thing you had going on for a while there."

"There was – still is – a lot to do at the clinic," she countered. "I'm taking it a little easier because of the pregnancy. Otherwise, I'd still be working those ridiculous hours. That had nothing to do with Bay."

"You pined for the male. Don't even try to deny it."

"'Pined' is a strong word."

"And yet it's the right one." Drago sat back on the sofa and folded his arms.

"Okay fine, I'm not sure why but I did…feel something and, I guess, it translated into pining-like behavior but I'm not in love with him or anything. There's nothing between us."

"You pined and he fucked around. He may not have had sex with anyone, but the dragon was at that rut weekend." Drago made a disgusted face.

"Yeah, but like you pointed out, he didn't have sex with anyone."

"He almost did. Came very close. And he was there in the first place, wasn't he?" Drago was saying all the things she had been thinking. Still was thinking.

"It's over between us, we're going to raise this child as a couple and that's where it will end." She shook her head. "Please stop being hard on him. You are going to have to work with him and—"

"No, I'm not! He won't make the Elite team." Drago looked animated. "Not if I have anything to say about it."

"Brant told me that Bay has fantastic skills. He is also calm under pressure and intelligent as well."

Drago snorted.

"He isn't a bad guy, I swear."

"Are you sure you don't have feelings for him?"

She shrugged, not wanting to lie.

"Great!" he groaned.

"I won't act on them. Not after everything. Besides, I don't think he feels the same. He's here for the baby." She picked up one of the cushions from the sofa and hugged it to her chest.

"Still. Living with someone you could end up falling in love with is risky."

"I don't have a choice here. I won't act on it," she assured him again. "With that in mind, I need blood please."

Her stomach churned. Thing was, she didn't want Drago's blood, she wanted Bay's. Not a good idea though, given that the act would be sexual since they were so attracted to each other.

Drago lifted his brows. "You're tempted to drink from the dragon."

She nodded. "And if I drink from him…"

"You guys will end up rutting," Drago stated the obvious.

She looked down at her lap. "That's what I'm afraid of. His scent is growing more appealing by the day."

"His scent or him?" Drago asked, his eyes on her.

"Both, I guess." There was no guessing required. It was stupid of her. Stupid but true.

"I'm worried about you." Drago turned to her. "I'm worried you're going to get hurt. That the two of you will end up together for all the wrong reasons. You might just live to regret it."

"I know. That's why I need some of your blood. I'll stay two steps ahead of this."

"If you're sure?"

"I'm fine. I might need to drink from you a little more regularly though." Even if it wasn't what she wanted.

"Of course. Any time." He held out his arm.

"Even though I can't return the favor." They decided it would be better if Drago didn't drink from her again, on account of her blood was becoming addictive to him. Same as Bay's had become to her. It seemed that dragon blood was pretty hectic to vampires. Drago wouldn't admit it, but he was struggling after going cold turkey.

"Of course." He smiled, but she could see the tightness in his jaw.

"I'm sorry." She narrowed her eyes into his.

"It's for the best." Drago pretended to play it cool, but she could see the tension in him.

"You're the best friend a girl could ask for." She took his arm.

"You know it," Drago said, winking at her.

Ceri sank her teeth into his skin just as the door opened and Bay walked in. He stopped in his tracks, his smile dying on his face. Bay roared just before he attacked.

CHAPTER 23

H e was excited to finish practice early. Zane had told them to take the rest of the day off. The others had been just as excited as he was. Zane was normally a hard-ass about practicing. Who was he to look a gift horse in the mouth?

Bay planned to ask Ceri if she wanted to go to lunch with him. It was her day off. She didn't get many of those and he wanted to make the most of it.

He could sense she was apprehensive to explore anything further between them. She was still attracted to him. Possibly even as much as he was to her. Ceri had been gorgeous before, she was unbelievably sexy now. All beautiful soft curves. He knew without a doubt that he wanted her, and he hoped and prayed that she felt the same way. He hadn't tried to make any moves. Maybe today was the day. He wanted to push for something small, like holding her hand maybe. They had to start somewhere. He had to convince her that a real relationship was the way to go. It felt right to him.

It probably wasn't a good idea to rush into sex. Although compatibility was important in any relationship, it wasn't everything. Not by a long shot.

He needed to convince her there could be more

between them. He was feeling more, at least from his side. The shared meals, the laughs. He touched her belly at any chance he got, still couldn't believe he was going to be a father. He couldn't think of anyone he'd rather have as his kid's mother. Ceri was going to be an amazing mom.

Bay was going to suggest that they go into town. They needed a ton of things for the baby. Clothing, a stroller, a crib. He'd been doing some research on newborns. In less than three months the little one would be there, and they needed to be ready. After shopping, he would suggest lunch. He'd take Ceri somewhere nice – he'd already booked a restaurant, just in case. Call him an optimist.

Bay couldn't keep the smile off his face. He opened the front door, expecting to find her curled up on the couch with a good book.

His smile died instantly as his eyes locked with that asshole vampire. A smirk appeared on the male's face. He had his arm slung around Ceri's shoulders. *His female. His!* Ceri had her fangs in the soft flesh of Drago's arm. She pulled back, her eyes wide.

That's when he realized he'd growled. The sound low and fierce. Anger coiled in his belly. He'd made it clear that he was there if she wanted blood. Why was she taking from him?

The male's smirk grew. His arm tightened around her in a possessive fashion.

Fuck that!

He growled again. He couldn't help it. This asshole was getting on his last nerve.

"Bay," Ceri said as he marched over to them. "Wait! What—?" she yelled as he grabbed Drago by the hair, hauling him to his feet.

"You don't get to touch her, fucker!" he snarled, his

voice deep and guttural. He wanted to pulverize Drago. Teach him a lesson once and for all.

Drago tried to punch him, but he blocked his fist. "She's not yours," the male retaliated. "You don't deserve her," he added with a sneer.

"Ceri is mine and it's about time you realized that."

Drago laughed. The asshole laughed in his face. Bay saw red. He punched the vampire...punched him hard. Not hard enough to break anything but it was close. The male would sport some bruises. Drago went flying, crashing into the dining room table. There was a crack as it splintered under his weight.

"Stop!" Ceri cried, grabbing his arm. "Don't! I asked him to come. I asked if I could drink from him. If you're going to get angry with someone, get angry with me."

"I told you, you could drink from me." It took everything in him to speak softly. "You don't need this asshole." He growled the last.

"This asshole happens to be my friend," she snapped back, eyes blazing. Her hands moving to her hips.

Drago stood up, he was rubbing his jaw. He gave a shake of his head. "I think you two have a couple of things you need to discuss." The male grinned.

Asshole!

Bay frowned. He hadn't expected that response. Truth be told, he thought he was going to have to fight. His hands were still curled up into tight fists. His muscles bunched. Bay's frown deepened as he watched the male leave.

"What the hell was that?" Ceri demanded. "I'm not yours. You're here for the baby, not for me."

"I'm here for both of you."

She shook her head. "Like hell! If it weren't for the

baby, you wouldn't be here. Admit it!"

"I haven't been able to get you off my mind since I first met you."

"Yeah, because you wanted a cure!" she yelled back.

"At first, I thought that was the case, but I was wrong. I couldn't get you off my mind after I had been cured. If anything, it was worse."

"Bullshit!" Her eyes were blazing. "That's why you felt the need to go on one of those rut weekends…because you couldn't stop thinking about me." She looked pissed.

"My friend, Beck, had me over a barrel, I had to go. It was either I go along, or the Stag Run would be canceled. The Stag Run is very important for morale amongst the males."

"I'll bet." She snorted. "And while you were there, you thought you'd just get in on the action."

"You're jealous. You realize that, don't you?"

"Oh, please." She made a face. "I'm calling you out on your bullshit, that's all!" She put her hands on her hips and glared at him.

"I missed you more once I was in Beachhaven. Everything reminded me of you, so I decided to head to our bar. I wasn't having any fun watching the males pair off. I became angry because I pictured you moving on with your life and that's when I decided to—"

"Find out if that blonde was blonde everywhere?" Her jaw was tight. Her eyes narrowed.

Shit! Why did she have to hear that? "I couldn't go through with it. We left five minutes after that. I ended up putting her in the Uber – alone. I headed back to my place – alone. I didn't so much as kiss her, let alone do anything else. I knew right then and there that I wasn't going to be able to forget you. It didn't matter how many weeks, or months or years for that matter, went by. I knew you would still be on my mind. Screwing someone else would make no difference. I planned on confronting you, I swear! Only, you were there first. You beat me to it. This happened." He looked down at her slightly rounded belly. "Now you think I'm only here for our child, and that's not true."

Ceri shook her head, her eyes were wide.

"You have to believe me."

"I want to believe you, but I'm struggling. It would be wrong of us to get together just because of this child. We would regret it."

"It wouldn't just be for the child." Bay cupped her jaw. He let his thumb graze the side of her cheek. "I swear. Just admit you have feelings for me too and we can take it from there. One step at a time. As slow or as fast as you want."

She finally nodded. Her green eyes so vivid. Bay leaned in and pressed his lips to hers. They were soft. They were amazing lips. As much as he wanted to devour her mouth, he kept it soft and tender, not wanting to scare her off. Then came the pinch as his tongue scraped one of her fangs. Ceri moaned. She pulled back, her fangs were long and sharp. Her eyes...beautiful. The green was tinged with red. She hissed as she sank her fangs into his neck. Bay grunted, his cock becoming rigid in a second.

Ceri gripped his shoulders, pressing her body against his. Pleasure surged through him. The need to rut made his eyes water and his jaw clench. She released him, her eyes were hazy.

"I want you," she said, her voice laced with desperation.

Bay swallowed and nodded. They were good together. He needed to remind her of that. He gripped the bottom of her shirt and tugged it up. Ceri lifted her arms.

She was wearing a white, cotton bra. Her breasts were

much fuller. "Beautiful," he murmured as he cupped them through the fabric.

She pulled her tights down, looking as frantic as he was feeling. She was a thing of beauty. "So sexy," he whispered as he pulled his own pants off. Admiring, the deep curves of her breasts and the roundness of her belly. The added softness to her hips.

Bay took back her mouth. This time he did plunder. He did devour and by the little noises she was making and the way she rubbed herself on his dick, he could tell that she was enjoying it.

Ceri could still taste him on her lips. This time she got all of the potency, all of the richness and none of the terrible burn. Her nipples instantly hardened. Her boobs felt full and tender. Her channel turned slick. There was this zing of intense need that rushed between her legs as she slid her fangs free.

She was aching. So ready for him it was a joke. It wouldn't take much to finish her. Bay tugged on her bra, taking the straps down and freeing her breasts. His eyes turned hazy with desire. Bay leaned down, taking one of her nipples into his mouth and sucking softly.

They were sensitive, but it felt so darned good that she moaned. "I need you now." She was panting.

Bay nodded. "I haven't been with anyone else." Then his eyes flashed with panic.

"Neither have I," she blurted, seeing a look of relief cross his face.

Bay's grip on her hips tightened, he turned her around, so that she was facing the back of the sofa.

Ceri put her hands on the chair back, using it as a

purchase. She opened her legs, feeling him move between them. "Don't want to harm you or—"

"You won't," she said, sounding desperate.

Bay rubbed on her clit a few times. Ceri cried out, then he slid a finger inside her. "Wet for me," he murmured.

He lined up his cock, pushing inside her using slow, easy strokes. It only took a couple and he was inside her to the hilt. She whimpered, and he grunted. "So fucking amazing," he ground out as he pulled back.

Ceri could feel he was shaking a little. He kept the thrusts slow and even. He reached around and cupped her breasts, then he slid a hand down her body, over her belly and sought out her clit. He kept his touch soft.

Ceri cried out. "More!" she groaned. "Please."

Bay thrust a little harder, he picked up the pace. Groaning or grunting with each push. His finger stayed soft, slipping and sliding over her clit.

"Oh god! Oh yes…" She could feel everything pulling tight. She squeezed her eyes shut as the first waves of pleasure hit.

Bay grunted, thrusting harder. He rubbed her clit harder and faster as well. Her orgasm hit just as hard and fast. It had been a long time. Too long. Her body had been craving this male, not just for the past week but for months.

His big body crouched over her and he groaned long and deep as he gave in to his release. He finally slowed, closing his arms around her in an embrace. They were both breathing hard.

Now that she had come, she could think a little more rationally. "We maybe shouldn't have done that."

Bay pulled out of her, turning her so that she faced him. "Of course we should have done that."

"We let the need for sex cloud our judgment. It's clear that we're compatible. We're very attracted to one another. The sex is amazing but that doesn't mean we belong together."

"I love being inside you." Bay's eyes were locked with hers. "Love it! I know that I could fuck fifty females and not feel what I feel when I'm with you."

"See, that's what I—"

"Let me finish. I also happen to enjoy spending time with you," Bay said. "I enjoy talking about your day. Cooking you dinner. I want to go shopping for the baby now. That's why I rushed home. I booked us in for lunch at one of the fancy restaurants in town. They apparently specialize in barbecue. Thought you might like a steak or some lamb chops."

He was being super sweet. Super thoughtful. "You're not just saying and doing this for the baby, are you? Because I would never keep you from our child. You don't have to—"

Bay shook his head. "I want to be with you. I have feelings for you. They're real. I'm very serious about you and it has nothing to do with the baby. I planned on seeing you again, on convincing you that we should give us a chance. Now I have to convince you that I mean it but that's okay. I'm fine with that."

She felt her heart squeeze and her eyes fill with tears. The hormones, she was blaming it on them.

"Are you willing to try?" His eyes were filled with such hope.

"Yes. I am." She smiled, it suddenly felt like a weight lifted.

Bay kissed her, hard and deep. He finally released her, pulling back. "What do you say we go shopping for a crib and diapers?"

"I say, let's go in a half an hour." She reached forward and palmed his cock. "It has been a very long time."

"You come up with such fantastic ideas." Bay grinned, looking gorgeous.

"I know I do." She reached up and kissed him.

CHAPTER 24

One month later…

"You're sure?" Zane frowned so hard it was comical. Bay held back a laugh. The vampire king would not appreciate being laughed at. "I'm very sure. Thank you for making the offer. I don't enjoy being a warrior though." He shook his head.

"But you're one of the best I have ever seen," Zane countered, still frowning heavily.

"Just because a person is good at something, doesn't mean they enjoy doing it. It's taken me a long time to come to that conclusion and here I am."

"Okay. If you change your—"

"I doubt it, my lord. Thank you again."

Zane nodded once.

"Oh, and congratulations on the birth of your son." Bay smiled.

Zane's face lit up, the male beamed. "Thank you. We are very happy. Zackery is doing very well. He is healthy and strong. He has already put on two pounds."

"Wonderful. I believe he looks exactly like you."

Zane nodded. "He has my eyes, loves drinking from Tanya and sleeps very well."

"What does Sammy think of his little brother?"

"Loves him, maybe a little too much. Sam keeps trying to take him out of the stroller or the crib. He almost dropped him the other day." Zane shook his head. "We have to watch him like a hawk. With that in mind, I am going home to visit with my family."

"Good idea! They grow up so fast. In less than two months I'll be a father as well." he shook his head. "I can't believe how quickly time is flying."

"Yes, I am told that Ceri is doing well."

"Yes, she is." Bay was sure he had the same beaming look Zane had been sporting not a minute ago.

They walked out of Zane's office together. The king hurried off towards the castle. Drago was waiting outside. He slapped Bay on the back. "So, are congratulations in order? Did you make the Elite team?"

"I made the team but—"

"Yeah!" Drago yelled. "I knew you would do it. You're close to unbeatable in—"

"Hold up!" Bay chuckled. "Just a second," he added when he saw that Drago wasn't listening, "I turned it down."

"What?" Drago's eyes widened. "What do you mean you turned it down? No-one turns down a chance to be an Elite. Are you crazy?"

"I guess I must be, because I turned it down."

"What are you going to do then?" Drago shook his head. He looked just as shocked as Zane had.

Bay shrugged. "For now, I'm going to give my soon-to-be mate a helping hand."

"Yeah, Ceri could do with some help." Drago nodded. "She is on her feet far too much."

"I'll do all the grunt work. Help where I can so that she

can take it easy."

"You are a good male," Drago said. "I'm glad I got the two of you together. If it weren't for me, you guys would still be pussyfooting around one another."

"And I can't thank you enough." Drago had orchestrated the whole thing. He'd organized with Zane that Bay would be let off work early so that he would catch Ceri drinking from Drago. Bay had acted exactly as Drago had expected. Jealous and possessive as hell, and the rest was history.

"Do you need me to intervene so that Ceri finally agrees to mate you?" Drago asked. "I'm sure I could think of something that would hurry her along."

Bay chuckled. "No! Thank you for caring but we'll figure it out. Ceri will agree to mate me when she is good and ready."

"If you're sure."

"I am." Bay nodded.

"By the way, the curiosity is killing me. I know you told Ceri the full details, but she refuses to say anything about it." Drago shuffled his feet.

"Yes?" Bay prompted when he didn't continue.

"What happened to you? Your dick that is – she said it was severed in an accident and that silver was involved but she refuses to tell me anything else about it."

Bay smiled. "Ceri tells me that you are a male slut. I think that's what she calls you."

Drago smiled. "Not so much anymore."

"Good! Then hopefully what happened to me won't happen to you. I was dating a she-dragon. She was obviously way more serious about things than I was. I decided to go into town on the Stag Run."

"On a rut weekend." Drago widened his eyes. "It

doesn't sound like those have been very good to you; aside from the one where you met Ceri, that is. Go on," the male prompted.

"I was feeling the pressure to settle down and was nowhere near ready. Anyway, I was about to bed a human when she walked in on us. Ember was so pissed off. She saw red, grabbed a knife, the blade was silver-plated. Before I knew it…" He made a sweeping motion at his crotch area.

Drago groaned. "No! She didn't!"

"She most certainly did. It grew back but didn't work."

"Not at all?"

"No, not until Ceri drank from me."

"Interesting." Drago nodded. "I'm going to be more careful around females.

"Good idea," Bay said. "I'm heading to the clinic now."

"By the way, I'm joining you guys for dinner tonight," Drago said.

"I thought you were meeting human females as a part of that whole program you guys are running."

"Nah," Drago shook his head, "I changed my mind."

"Okay." Bay shrugged. "We'll see you later then."

"What are you doing here?" Ceri looked at her watch and then back at Bay. "Did you finish early?"

"Nope." Bay shook his head. He leaned down and kissed her, first on the lips and then on the forehead. "I'm only just starting my day actually."

"Well, then what are doing here?" Ceri asked again.

"I'm here to help you."

She frowned. "Wait, weren't you supposed to hear whether or not you got the Elite position? Wait a minute."

She pushed her chair back, standing up. "Don't tell me you didn't get it. That you worked so hard to prove yourself for nothing. That you did prove yourself and then didn't get it. I'm going to go and talk to Brant…after my next appointment that is. Zane had better have a damned good explanation as to why you were not appointed. It's because you're a dragon, isn't it?"

Bay was smiling at her. He shook his head. His eyes were bright and beautiful in the morning light. He looked the picture of calm, not like someone who had just been disappointed. "What is it?"

"I turned it down."

"What? Why?" she asked, eyebrows raised.

"It's not what I want."

"Why not? I thought you…" She frowned as realization hit. "Do you want to go back to your lair? Would you prefer to—"

"No," he shook his head, still smiling, "I've never enjoyed being a warrior. I hate leading teams into battle and the endless perimeter patrols. All of the skills training is a ball-ache. I want to do something different, and right now that 'something different' is helping you. I don't want you on your feet so much. I don't want you lifting heavy equipment."

"Oh." She sat back down. "You want to help out around here."

He nodded.

"Um…you're a male."

"Is that a problem? I don't think it's a problem." Bay shook his head. "You keep saying how you want to see more males in traditionally female roles. Well, here I am."

"Are you sure though? I help females give birth. I counsel in the use of birth control and safe sex. I—"

"I know." Bay nodded. "You've told me a lot about what you do. I'm here and I want to help. I'm not sure it's something I'll do for forever, but right now…yes, I'm interested. If you'll have me."

"I suppose I *have* talked a lot about my work. And you're certain you'd—"

"Very." He walked behind her and started massaging her shoulders. She made a moaning noise just as Lily walked in.

"Oh." Her mouth formed an O. "Am I interrupting?"

"Not at all," Ceri blurted.

Bay stopped massaging her.

"In fact, you're right on time. This is Bay." Ceri gestured to the father of her child, her boyfriend, her soon-to-be so much more.

Lily smiled. "Hello, I've heard all about you."

"Bay meet Lily."

He leaned forward and shook her hand. "Hi."

"I hope you don't mind, but Bay will be working as my assistant for the coming period." She couldn't believe it, but he seemed sincere about wanting this. She half expected him to run at the first sign of blood.

"Not at all." Lily shook her head. "Good to meet you."

"Okay, so, any news for me?" Ceri asked.

Lily shook her head, her eyes were clouded, her shoulders slumped. "I'm afraid not."

"When was the last time you took a pregnancy test?"

"Last week. It's just too depressing seeing a single line."

"I understand." Ceri opened the drawer, taking a box out. "I think the first order of business is to do one." She handed the box to Lily. She didn't have to tell the other female where the bathroom was.

Lily nodded and disappeared behind the closed door.

"I really hope it's positive this time," Ceri said.

"How long have Lily and her mate been trying to become pregnant?"

"Going on three years now," Ceri said. "I feel a bit guilty." She rubbed her growing bump. It was well-rounded and easy to see she was pregnant but at the same time very neat and tidy. If she didn't get too much bigger, she would probably be able to birth this child.

"You have nothing to feel guilty about," Bay said, looking at her head-on.

"I know." She sighed. "It's just, here I was, not trying— heck I didn't even know I could become pregnant – and boom!"

"We dragons have potent seed." He winked at her.

Ceri laughed. "Yeah right. So, I have some news."

"Yes?" Bay narrowed his eyes in interest.

"Our new house is ready. We can move in at the weekend." She made a squealing noise to show how excited she was.

"We get to finally decorate the nursery." Bay grinned. "We'll go shopping on Saturday."

"Sounds like a plan."

Just then, the door opened and Lily came out, holding the test in her hand. Ceri knew what the outcome was just by looking at her facial expression. "Negative?" she asked, feeling bad for the female.

Lily nodded. "That damned single line again. I know I'm pregnant. I just know it, and yet, I won't be able to relax until I know for sure. It's so frustrating."

"You said your menstruation was very light last month?"

"Yes, that's right." Lily nodded.

"Any other symptoms?" Ceri asked.

"No." She shook her head. "My breasts aren't as tender as they were." Again, the slumping of the shoulders.

"And Stuart hasn't been able to hear a heartbeat?"

Lily shook her head. "He presses his ear to my belly every single evening without fail and still nothing.

"I have a stethoscope, we can try that. The heartbeat is most likely still too faint for the naked ear to hear."

"Oh, that would be great. I would really appreciate it." Lily's voice became animated.

"I must warn you that it is probably still too early even with a stethoscope."

"It would be great if we could try." Lily nodded, her ponytail bobbed.

"Okay then," Ceri said. "Let's go over there. You can sit on the gurney." She opened another drawer on her desk and pulled out the stethoscope.

Lily did as she was told.

"Lie down and pull your shirt up a bit. That's it."

Bay stood to the side, observing. She caught his gaze. "Let me know if you need me to help with anything." He winked at her.

"I will." She smiled back.

Ceri put the earpieces into her ears and placed the diaphragm on Lily's stomach. She moved the bell around, taking her time to listen. Ceri kept repositioning the diaphragm, trying again and again. Aside from the normal noises, she couldn't hear anything.

"It's not working, is it?" Lily sounded disappointed.

"I'm so sorry. Give it another two weeks and then we'll know for sure. I know it's hard to wait but—"

"Let me try," Bay interjected.

"Um…"

"Dragons have much better hearing than vampires.

Maybe I can pick up a heartbeat." He shrugged his big shoulders.

Ceri looked at Lily who nodded. "Yes, why not. You never know."

"Okay." Ceri took the earpieces out and handed the stethoscope to Bay, who went through the same motions as she had earlier.

He repositioned the diaphragm several times until he finally sucked in a deep breath, standing up. He was grinning.

"And?" Ceri felt her heart beating faster. There weren't many vampire females who were capable of giving birth to a baby. Many of those struggled to get pregnant in the first place. Any pregnancy was considered a miracle and a blessing since they were so rare.

Lily was holding her breath; her face was white and her eyes wide.

"I heard it, the unmistakable sound of a second, much softer, much faster heartbeat."

Ceri screamed with excitement. Lily clapped a hand to her mouth. She laughed but was crying at the same time. "Are you sure?" she finally managed to get out.

"Yes, very sure." Bay was still grinning. "Congratulations."

"Oh my god," Lily squealed. "I can't believe it. I can't!" She sat up. "I knew it! I told Stuart to come today but he didn't want to jinx it." She laughed some more through her tears.

"That was awesome and it's only my first day." Bay put his arm around her. "This was so much fun!"

"Well," Ceri took Bay's hand, "it looks like you might be a keeper."

"I hope you're not just talking about as an assistant."

He narrowed his eyes.

"I most definitely am not just talking about as an assistant."

"Good." Bay leaned in and kissed her.

Ceri pretended to smack him on the arm when he pulled back. "No fraternizing on the job."

"Party pooper!" he kissed her again. When they came up for air Lily was gone and Ceri couldn't wipe the smile from her face.

CHAPTER 25

"**P**ush!" Meghan shouted.

One of the dragon shifter elders held her hand tightly. "You're okay, sweetie," she whispered. "You're doing great!"

It didn't feel like it. Ceri had been in labor for hours, more than she could count. She'd been pushing for what felt like forever. Her reserves were all but drained.

"It's a tight fit, but I know you can do this. You need to dig really deep," her doctor urged. "You ready?" Meghan had an encouraging smile and very kind eyes. Ceri had liked the human from the moment she had met her.

Ceri tried to nod. Had to work just to make that small movement. Right now, even breathing felt like an effort.

There was a commotion at the door. "I don't give a fuck!" It was Bay. Her mate sounded agitated. He'd been trying to gain entry for the last hour.

"Bay," she tried to scream, but it came out as a whisper. "Bay," she tried again.

The elder squeezed her hand. "You can do this."

"Move or I'm going to hurt you," Bay snarled. The door opened and then slammed shut again.

A male said something, she wasn't sure what because another pain was searing through her. She clenched her teeth. "No!" she moaned. "I can't. Not again!" Her throat felt dry.

"You can!" Meghan urged. "Breathe." Her doctor began mimicking the breathing technique. Ceri did the same.

Doctor Meghan looked between her legs. "Push!" she shouted.

Instead of doing what her doctor instructed, she slumped back. Her head was pounding, her lips felt dry and chapped. Her hair clung to her damp forehead. All she wanted to do was sleep; if not for the pain, she would.

"Don't fight the birthing pains," the elder urged. "You need to work with them. They are your friend."

Ceri wanted to snort. "No!" She shook her head.

"Move!" Bay yelled. There was a thudding noise of flesh on flesh, followed by a grunt and a hard bang. Then the door was flung open, knocking the wall and Bay strode into the room. "I'm here." He gripped her hand. "I'm not going anywhere." He growled the last, making sure everyone within hearing distance knew it.

"You should not be in—" the elder began.

"My mate needs me," Bay growled. "I am staying!"

She felt instantly better. Ceri tried to smile but another birth pain hit. This one more aggressive than the last. She ground her teeth together.

"Push, Ceri!" Meghan egged her on. "You need to give it everything."

Bay clutched her hand. "I wish I could do this for you." Ceri nodded.

"I love you and our baby so much. Please, my love, I need you to be strong." He leaned in and kissed her on the forehead.

Ceri nodded. *She could do this!* She had to do it. For their unborn child. For Bay. For herself. She pushed with everything she had. The pain seemed to last an age but she pushed and pushed and pushed, finally falling back on the pillow as it subsided. She made a noise of frustration.

"I saw the top of your baby's head." Meghan looked animated. "For just a second there."

Ceri had barely caught her breath and the next pain hit. She wanted to crunch forward. To scream. To—Bay squeezed her hand.

"Push, Ceri," he encouraged her.

"I can't," she sobbed.

"You must," Bay urged.

Ceri pushed. It was with all of her might. Everything she had, which wasn't much. She slumped back, trying to catch her breath. "Can't," she muttered. "Not working." She could barely get the words out. Could hardly keep her eyes open. The reprieve wasn't going to last.

"The baby keeps sucking back." Her doctor looked frustrated. "You're so close, Ceri. Just that little bit more. When the next one comes, you need to…"

Ceri shook her head, hot tears coursed down her cheeks. She had been strong for so long. She had reached a point where she just didn't have much left. She wished she could take a break. A proper break. A twenty-minute power nap or a—The next pains began to slice through her. Like she was being torn in two. She clutched her belly and moaned.

"Here," Bay held out his wrist to her, "drink. You need to—"

Ceri tried to lift her hand to clasp his wrist. It flopped uselessly at her side. "Here." Bay held his wrist to her lips.

Ceri bit down and his blood filled her mouth. She only took a few sips. She knew that too much would make her ill.

She could actually feel the blood enter her stomach, could feel how its energy began to surge through her. This time when Meghan screamed for her to push, she did. She gave it everything and more. A growl forming from deep inside her. She grit her teeth and clasped her thighs.

Ceri yelled as their child was born. The infant yelled even louder in the very next second.

"It's a boy!" Meghan shouted. "A healthy son."

"A boy." Bay beamed. Instead of looking at his son, his eyes were on her. "You did it, my love." He kissed her. "I love you so much."

"Love you too," she managed between pants.

"Here he is." Meghan held the little one.

"He's completely bald." Bay choked out a laugh, his eyes were glistening. "He has your eyes," he said as he took the squirming baby from Meghan. Their baby. Her little boy. Ceri realized that she was crying.

"He's perfect," Bay said, his voice hitching.

Ceri took her son and cradled him in her arms. He quietened down, looking up at her. "I'm your mom," she crooned. "It's nice to meet you," she managed between the tears.

She looked up at Doctor Meghan who was holding her own bump. The female was soon to be a mother herself. "Thank you," Ceri said.

Meghan nodded once and smiled. "He is beautiful. I'm so glad it all worked out."

"Me too," Ceri responded.

"Me three." Bay looked down at his son. His eyes filled with joy and wonder. "We're a family," he announced.

Ceri felt like her heart would burst.

CHAPTER 26

Alex crossed her legs, wanting to fill the silence. Her lips twitched with the need to do so. Instead, she bit down on the inside of her cheek to stop herself.

He who speaks first has lost.

Her father continued to stare her down. She felt like a little girl again. Wanting to squirm. Wanting to—

"And?" Angelo Bell folded his arms and leaned back in his chair. "Do you have the location of a lair? Have you captured one?"

Alex shook her head. "Not yet, I'm afraid. But—"

Her father sighed dramatically. "It might be time to bring in someone to help you. Harry Gunter would be the right candidate for the—"

"No!" she spat. Alex would rather die than work with that asshole.

"I know you two have a history but you will need to put your emotions aside. This is business, Alex. It's been over a year and you have nothing to show for it. You captured one but lost it. You hired thugs to do your bidding. The mission was a total failure." He touched his fingertips to the open file on his desk. "You are over budget and, if you ask me, in over your pretty, little head."

She pulled in a breath, trying to calm down. Why did

he have to refer to her looks all the time? What she looked like and the fact she didn't have a penis didn't make any difference. A fact she needed to prove over and over again, it would seem. It was growing tiresome.

"I will get the job done. I don't need Harry or anyone else." She was sure to keep her eyes on his. To keep her voice calm and even.

Do not show weakness.

"I have narrowed down the location of two of the lairs. The grid coordinates are noted in the file. We have spies in various regions in the US, with large rewards for any sightings. They are fully briefed on what to look for. I will follow up on a tip-off as soon we conclude this meeting. A couple meeting the criteria checked into a hotel in…" She hesitated. She didn't want to divulge any details in case her father sent Harry in behind her back. She wouldn't put it past him. Angelo Bell was ruthless. "All you need to know at this stage is that I have it fully under control and I will fly out straight after this meeting to follow up. You will be happy to note that it is a couple. The woman appears to be human, she is pregnant."

Her father's eye glinted and the one side of his mouth twitched. It wasn't very often that her father showed any kind of emotion. Within a split second, he was back to being stern and disapproving. "Don't disappoint me."

"I won't!"

"Good." He closed the file and handed it to her. "This is it, your last chance."

Her back stiffened as she rose to her feet. Then she nodded once and walked out the door. She immediately dialed the number she had been given. "Are they still there?" she barked into the phone.

"Yes," the woman replied. "Do I get my reward now?"

"Keep your eyes on them. Don't lose them. You get the reward when I get there."

"What if they leave? Or, even worse, check out?" She sounded panicked.

"Then all bets are off. Give me the details," Alex asked.

"I already—"

"I read the email, but I want to hear it from you," Alex interrupted, striding down the long hallway.

"They checked in as Meghan and Tide Smith."

Her heart beat faster. "Yes." She nodded, pushing the elevator button. A fueled jet was waiting for her at the airport. "And the woman is definitely pregnant?"

"Without a doubt. The guy is huge, bigger than any man I've ever seen. He looks like a bodybuilder or something. He has ice-blue eyes…they're freaky blue."

Excitement raced through her. The elevator doors opened. "What else?" Alex snapped.

"I saw what looked like a golden tattoo on his chest when he leaned over to pick something up."

"Don't lose them," Alex hissed.

"Okay, I won't. I need the money," the woman said.

"Then you know what to do. Not a word of this to anyone else."

"O-okay."

Alex ended the call as she got into the back of the waiting Mercedes. "Go!" she instructed her driver. "To the airport, as quick as you can." Her heart beat faster. If all went well, she would have a male dragon and his whelp for her father within the next twenty-four hours. Nothing was going to stand in her way.

AUTHOR'S NOTE

Charlene Hartnady is a USA Today Bestselling author. She loves to write about all things paranormal including vampires, elves and shifters of all kinds. Charlene lives on an acre in the country with her husband and three sons. They have an array of pets including a couple of horses.

She is lucky enough to be able to write full time, so most days you can find her at her computer writing up a storm. Charlene believes that it is the small things that truly matter like that feeling you get when you start a new book, or when you look at a particularly beautiful sunset.

BOOKS BY THIS AUTHOR

The Chosen Series:
Book 1 ~ Chosen by the Vampire Kings
Book 2 ~ Stolen by the Alpha Wolf
Book 3 ~ Unlikely Mates
Book 4 ~ Awakened by the Vampire Prince
Book 5 ~ Mated to the Vampire Kings (Short Novel)
Book 6 ~ Wolf Whisperer (Novella)
Book 7 ~ Wanted by the Elven King

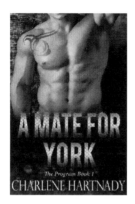

The Program Series (Vampire Novels):
Book 1 ~ A Mate for York
Book 2 ~ A Mate for Gideon
Book 3 ~ A Mate for Lazarus
Book 4 ~ A Mate for Griffin
Book 5 ~ A Mate for Lance
Book 6 ~ A Mate for Kai
Book 7 ~ A Mate for Titan

Shifter Night:
Book 1 ~ Untethered
Book 2 ~ Unbound
Book 3 ~ Unchained

The Feral Series
Book 1 ~ Hunger Awakened
Book 2 ~ Power Awakened

The Bride Hunt Series (Dragon Shifter Novels)
Book 1 ~ Royal Dragon
Book 2 ~ Water Dragon
Book 3 ~ Dragon King
Book 4 ~ Lightning Dragon
Book 5 ~ Forbidden Dragon
Book 6 ~ Dragon Prince

Demon Chaser Series (No cliffhangers):
Book 1 ~ Omega
Book 2 ~ Alpha
Book 3 ~ Hybrid
Book 4 ~ Skin
Demon Chaser Boxed Set Book 1–3

A MATE FOR YORK

The Program Book 1

CHARLENE HARTNADY

1

CASSIDY'S HANDS WERE CLAMMY and shaking. She had just retyped the same thing three times. At this rate, she would have to work even later than normal to get her work done. She sighed heavily.

Pull yourself together.

With shaking hands, she grabbed her purse from the floor next to her, reached inside and pulled out the folded up newspaper article.

Have you ever wanted to date a vampire?

Human women required. Must be enthusiastic about interactions with vampires. Must be willing to undergo a stringent medical exam. Must be prepared to sign a contractual agreement which would include a non-disclosure clause. This will be a temporary position. Limited spaces available within the program. Successful

*candidates can earn up to $45,000 per day, over a three-
day period.*

All she needed was three days leave.

Cassidy wasn't sure whether her hands were shaking because she had to ask for the leave and her boss was a total douche bag or because the thought of vampires drinking her blood wasn't exactly a welcome one.

More than likely a combination of both.

This was a major opportunity for her though. She had already been accepted into the trial phase of the program that the vampires were running. What was three days in her life? So there was a little risk involved. Okay, a lot of risk, but it would all be worth it in the end. She was drowning in debt. Stuck in a dead-end job. Stuck in this godforsaken town. This was her chance, her golden opportunity, and she planned on seizing it with both hands.

To remind herself what she was working towards, or at least running away from, she let her eyes roam around her cluttered desk. There were several piles of documents needing to be filed. A stack of orders lay next to her cranky old laptop. Hopefully it wouldn't freeze on her this time while she was uploading them into the system. It had been months since Sarah had left. There used to be two of them performing her job, and since her colleague was never replaced it was just her. She increasingly found that she had to get to work way earlier and stay later and later just to get the job done.

To add insult to injury, there were many days that her a-hole boss still had the audacity to come down on her for not meeting a deadline. He refused to listen to reason and would not accept being understaffed as an excuse. She'd never been one to shy away from hard work but the expectations were ridiculous. Her only saving grace was that she didn't have much of a life.

There had to be something more out there for her – and a hundred and thirty-five thousand big ones would not only pay off her debts but would also give her enough cash to go out and find one. A life, that is, and a damned good life it would be.

Cassidy took a deep breath and squared her shoulders. If she asked really nicely, hopefully Mark would give her a couple of days off. She couldn't remember the last time she had taken leave. Then it dawned on her, she'd taken three days after Sean had died a year ago. Her boss couldn't say no though. If he did, she wasn't beyond begging.

Rising to her feet, she made for the closed door at the other end of her office. After knocking twice, she entered.

The lazy ass was spread out on the corner sofa with his hands crossed behind his head. He didn't look in the least bit embarrassed about her finding him like that either.

"Cassidy." He put on a big cheesy smile as he rose to a sitting position. The buttons on his jacket pulled tight around his paunchy midsection. He didn't move much and ate big greasy lunches so it wasn't surprising. "Come on in. Take a seat," he gestured to a spot next to him on the sofa.

That would be the day. Her boss could get a bit touchy feely. Thankfully it had never gone beyond a pat on the butt, a hand on her shoulder or just a general invasion of her personal space. It put her on edge though because it was becoming worse of late. The sexual innuendos were also getting highly irritating. She pretended that they went over her head, but he was becoming more and more forward as time went by.

By the way his eyes moved down her body, she could tell that he was most definitely mentally undressing her. *Oh god.* That meant that he was in one of his grabby moods. *Damn.* She preferred it when he was acting like a total jerk. Easier to deal with.

"No, that's fine. Thank you." She worked hard to plaster a smile on her face. "I don't want to take up much of your time and I have to get back to work myself."

His eyes narrowed for a second before dropping to her breasts. "You could do with a little break every now and then... so could I for that matter." Even though she knew he couldn't see anything because of her baggy jacket, his eyes stayed glued to her boobs anyway. Why did she get the distinct impression that he was no longer talking about work? *Argh!*

"How long has your husband been gone now?" he asked, his gaze still locked on her chest. It made her want to fold her arms but she resisted the temptation.

None of your damned business.

"It's been a year now since Sean passed." She tried hard to look sad and mournful. The truth was, if the bastard wasn't already dead she would've killed him herself. Turned out that there were things about Sean that she hadn't known. In fact, it was safe to say that she'd been living with and married to a total stranger. Funny how those things tended to come out when a person died.

Her boss did not need to know this information though. So far, playing the mourning wife was the only thing that kept him from pursuing her further.

"What can I do for you?" His eyes slid down to the juncture at her thighs and she had to fight the urge to squeeze them tightly together. Even though temperatures outside were damn near scorching, she still wore stockings, skirt to mid-calf, a button-up blouse and a jacket. Nothing was revealing and yet he still looked at her like she was standing there naked. It made her skin crawl. "I would be happy to oblige you. Just say the word, baby."

She hated it when he called her that. He started doing it a couple of weeks ago. Cassidy had asked him on several occasions to stop but she may as well have been speaking to a plank of wood.

She grit her teeth for a second, holding back a retort. "Great. Glad to hear it." Her voice sounded way more confident than she felt. "I need a couple of days off. It's been a really long time—"

"Forget it," he interrupted while standing up. "I need you… here." Another innuendo. Although she waited, he didn't give any further explanations.

"Look, I know there is a lot to do around here especially since Sarah left." His eyes clouded over immediately at the mention of her ex-colleague's name. "I would be happy to put in extra time."

As in, she wouldn't sleep and would have to work weekends to get the job done.

"I'll do whatever it takes. I just really need a couple of days. It's important."

His eyes lit up and she realized what she had just said and how it would've sounded to a complete pig like Mark.

"Anything?" he rolled the word off of his tongue.

"Well…" It came out sounding breathless but only because she was nervous. "Not anything. What I meant to say was—"

"No, no. I like that you would do anything, in fact, there is something I've been meaning to discuss with you." His gaze dropped to her breasts again.

Please no. Anything but that.

Cassidy swallowed hard, actually feeling sick to her stomach. She shook her head.

"You can have a few days, baby. In fact, I'll hire you an assistant." Ironically he played with the wedding band on his ring finger. His voice had turned sickly sweet. "I'd be willing to go a long way for you if you only met me halfway. It's time you got over the loss of your husband and I plan on helping you to do that."

"Um… I don't think…" Her voice was soft and shaky. Her hands shook too, so she folded her arms.

This was not happening.

"Look, Cass… baby, you're an okay-looking woman. Not normally the type I'd go for. I prefer them a bit younger, bigger tits, tighter ass…" He looked her up and down as if he were sizing her up and finding her lacking. "I'd be willing to give you a go… help you out. Now… baby…" he paused.

Cassidy felt like the air had seized in her lungs, like her heart had stopped beating. Her mouth gaped open but she couldn't close it. She tried to speak but could only manage a croak.

She watched in horror as her boss pulled down his zipper and pulled out a wrinkled, flaccid cock. "Suck on this. Or you could bend over and I'll fuck you – the choice is yours. I would recommend the fuck because quite frankly I think you could use it." He was deadly serious. Even gave a small nod like he was doing her a favor or something.

To the delight of her oxygen starved lungs, she managed to suck in a deep breath but still couldn't get any words out. Not a single, solitary syllable.

"I know you've had to play the part of the devastated wife and all that but I'm sure you really want a bit of this." He waved his cock at her, although wave was not the right description. The problem was that a limp dick couldn't really wave. It flopped about pathetically in his hand.

Cassidy looked from his tiny dick up to his ruddy, pasty face and back down again before bursting out laughing. It was the kind of laugh that had her bending at the knees, hunching over. Sucking in another lungful of air, she gave it all she had. Unable to stop even if she wanted to. Until tears rolled down her cheeks. Until she was gasping for breath.

"Hey now…" Mark started to look distinctly uncomfortable. "That's not really the sort of response I expected from you." He didn't look so sure anymore, even started to put his dick away before his eyes hardened.

Cassidy wiped the tears from her face. She still couldn't believe what the hell she was seeing and even worse, what she was hearing. *What a complete asshole.*

Her boss took a step towards her. "The time for games is over. Get down on your knees if you want to keep your job. I'm your boss and your behavior is just plain rude."

Any hint of humor evaporated in an instant. "I'll tell you what's rude… you taking out your thing is rude. You're right, you're my boss which means what is happening right here," she gestured between the two of them, looking pointedly at his member, "is called sexual harassment."

He narrowed his eyes at her. "Damn fucking straight, little missy. I want you to sexually harass this right now." He clutched his penis, flopping it around some more.

"Alrighty then. Let me just go and fetch my purse," she grinned at him, putting every little bit of sarcasm she had into the smile.

"Why would you need your purse?" he frowned.

"To get my magnifying glass. You have just about the smallest dick that I've ever seen." Not that she had seen many, but she didn't think she needed to. His penis was a joke.

It was his turn to gape. To turn a shade of bright red. "You didn't just say that. I'm going to pretend that I didn't hear that. This is your last fucking chance." Spittle flew from his mouth. "Show me your tits and get onto your fucking knees. Make me fucking come and do it now or you are out of a job."

"You can pretend all you want. As far as I'm concerned you can pretend that I'm sucking on your limp dick as well, because it will never happen. You can take your job and your tiny penis and shove um where the sun don't shine!" Cassidy almost wanted to slap a hand over her mouth, she couldn't believe that she had just said all of that. One thing was for sure, she was done taking shit from men. *Done!*

She gave him a disgusted look, turned on her heel and walked out. After grabbing her purse, she left without looking back, praying that her old faithful car would start. It hadn't been serviced since before her husband had died and it wasn't sounding right lately. The gearbox grated sometimes when she changed gears. There was a rattling noise. She just didn't have the funds. That was all about to change though. She hadn't exactly planned on leaving her job just yet. What if things didn't work out? She'd planned on keeping her job as a safety net instead of counting chickens she didn't have. It was too late to go back now.

Despite her lack of a backup plan, Cassidy grinned as her car started with a rattle and a splutter. Grinned even wider as she pulled away, hearing the gravel crunch beneath her tires. Now all she had to do was get through the next few days and she was home free.

Read it now!

Printed in Great Britain
by Amazon

48771575R00132